LETTERS FROM LAURA AND EVELINE

Fanny and Stella.

LETTERS

from

LAURA and EVELINE

GIVING AN ACCOUNT OF THEIR

Mock-Marriage, Wedding Trip

ETC.

Edited with an introduction and notes by
JUSTIN O'HEARN

VALANCOURT BOOKS

Letters from Laura and Eveline
Originally privately printed, London, 1883
This edition reprinted from the privately printed 1903 edition
First Valancourt Books edition 2013
First paperback edition 2015

Introduction and notes © 2013 by Justin O'Hearn
This edition © 2013 by Valancourt Books

Published by Valancourt Books, Richmond, Virginia
Publisher & Editor: JAMES D. JENKINS
http://www.valancourtbooks.com

ISBN 978-1-939140-71-5 (*hardcover*)
ISBN 978-1-941147-57-3 (*trade paper*)

Set in Dante MT 12/15

CONTENTS

CONTENTS

INTRODUCTION

There is a boldness in the idea upon which are based the two letters comprised in this volume, which, in spite of its monstrosity, might, with an abler and more delicate treatment, have lent itself to the creation of an attractive narrative. Conceptions equally impossible and contrary to the laws of nature have been productive of readable stories. Laura and Eveline are hermaphrodites, capable of enjoyment both active and passive, and they recount the incidents of their weddings, which take place simultaneously. Their husbands are neither astonished nor displeased at finding their brides endowed with the attributes of their own as well as of the softer sex. After these details, as disgusting as they are absurd, follows the description of an orgie, still more filthy and impossible, enacted by numerous ladies and gentlemen, at a London club, in honour of the said nuptials. The work, which is from the pen of its publisher, is mainly remarkable for its gross obscenity both in idea and language, and possesses no literary merit whatever.*

Henry Spencer Ashbee's lambasting of *Letters from Laura and Eveline* in his *Bibliography of Prohibited Books* (1885) is harsh. In pointing out just how bad *Letters* is, however, he unknowingly gives future readers and scholars all the more reason to seek this volume out. His claim that "it possesses no literary merit whatever" is undone by the fact that *Letters* exemplifies clandestinely published pornographic texts and print culture which reached a zenith in the late Victorian period. Pornographic publishing, especially in the late Victorian period, was a well-established business that operated parallel to mainstream publishing. By the time of *Letters* (1883) the industry had grown significantly, especially in London, where many booksellers had a robust trade in such material. This was particularly true of the famous 'Booksellers Row' in Holywell Street where, by the time Queen Victoria ascended the

---

* Pisanus Fraxi (pseudonym of Henry Spencer Ashbee), *Bibliography of Prohibited Books, Vol. 3: Catena Librorum Tacendorum* (1885), p. 403.

British throne in 1837, there were a number of booksellers there dealing in part or entirely in pornographic texts.

Ashbee is not wrong in his criticisms of the text; the orgies depicted *are* absurd. In fact, the entire book is absurd to the extent that its author and publisher cannot have been unaware of the fact. Ashbee's claim of *Letters'* absence of literary merit is based solely on the content of the book rather than taking into account its place within the larger context of Victorian pornography and print culture. He cannot be blamed for this critical oversight since he was a collector of Victorian pornography and wrote about it without the benefit of the hindsight modern readers and critics take for granted.

The subtitle of *Letters—Giving an Account of their Mock-Marriage, Wedding Trip, etc.—*tells readers what to expect within its pages as it builds on allusions to its predecessor, *The Sins of the Cities of the Plain* (1881). The earlier text, which contains the supposedly true memoir of Jack Saul, a Victorian 'mary-ann'* in London, introduces many of the settings, such as private sex clubs, and characters that appear in *Letters*. In a further subtitle, *Letters* is claimed to have been "Published as an Appendix to the Sins of the Cities", even though readers of *Sins* would be hard-pressed to find many similarities apart from the few character names and settings. This leads back to Ashbee's initial criticism that the book is "mainly remarkable for its gross obscenity", of which there is an abundance.

Background of *Laura and Eveline*: The Boulton and Park Affair and Jack Saul

The titular Laura and Eveline first appear in *Sins*, privately printed in 1881 and supposedly the life of the 'mary-ann' Jack Saul. The evidence that someone named Jack Saul wrote *Sins* is insufficient and it is more likely that he may have merely been the inspiration for the work rather than its author if he, in fact, even existed.† In *Sins*, Laura first appears as Ernest Boulton, one half

---

* A derogatory term for a male prostitute who dresses as a female.
† There is also some question about the identity of Jack Saul himself and whether he was a real person or became something of a code word for homosexuality in Victorian London.

of the real-life pair of cross-dressing men who were arrested in London's West End in April 1870 for "conspiring to commit [the] felony" of sodomy.* 'Conspiring' was a conveniently non-specific term exploitable by Victorian legislators and law enforcement but it suffices to say that, in this case and others, it meant sex with other men. This felony was known under the Offences Against the Person Act of 1861 as "the abominable crime of buggery" and carried at the time a penalty of "penal servitude for life or for any term not less than ten years".† Boulton's partner, Frederick Park, was known as Fanny in real life but Selina in both *Sins* and *Letters*.

Boulton and Park were well known in the West End for dressing up in ladies' clothing and playing ladies in independent theatre productions. Even though there "could be no doubt that all the defendants [especially Boulton and Park] were homosexuals"‡ the prosecution was unable to prove any actual crime or conspiracy to commit one by any of the parties involved in the indictment, and few lurid details of London's underground homosexual culture were revealed.

Boulton and Park stood trial in 1871 for their conspiracy to commit sodomy and the prosecution had Boulton and Park physically examined by a police surgeon in an attempt to prove anal intercourse had taken place. The medical 'evidence' was inconclusive and did not sway the proceedings to a guilty verdict, so Boulton and Park were acquitted.

The trial garnered immense attention in the newspapers as it implicated Member of Parliament Lord Arthur Clinton, who lived in the same lodgings as Boulton and Park,§ among other noblemen named in the indictment. Louis Charles Hurt, the "Louis H—" the epistles in *Letters* are addressed to, was a friend of Boulton and Park, had shared lodgings with them, and was implicated only because correspondence between him and the accused was

---

* See Hyde, *The Cleveland Street Scandal*, p. 96.
† Hyde, *The Other Love*, p. 92.
‡ *Ibid*, p. 96.
§ Hyde, *Cleveland*, p. 94.

found during a police search.* Lord Arthur was also implicated via correspondence in which Boulton had signed off 'Stella Clinton' and wrote as though (s)he were Lord Arthur's wife. Lord Arthur would never stand trial, however, having died the day after receiving his subpoena to appear in court. The cause of his death was reportedly scarlet fever, but it was actually suicide.

Eveline, as readers may well know, is the name given to Jack Saul in *Sins* when he is introduced into the world of the private homosexual clubs at a place called Inslip's as the guest of his client (or John, to use the modern parlance) Mr. Ferdinand.† However, Saul's was a name that gained notoriety by way of another sex scandal, the Cleveland Street Affair of 1889. A man calling himself Jack Saul was the star witness and gave damaging testimony about the men he had personally escorted to a male brothel at 19 Cleveland Street in London's west end. In doing so Saul incriminated himself on the stand and offered that he made his living as a "professional sodomite"‡ though he would never be charged with any crime from his admissions. Saul's testimony actually indicated that the London police turned a blind eye to his, and others', sexually dissident actions. Upon his confession that he still earned a living as a professional Mary-Ann he was asked whether he had been "hunted out by the police" to which he responded that they hadn't "interfered" with him and had to "shut their eyes to more than [just him]" within the underground community of which he was a significant participant.§

Saul is an intriguing figure for many reasons, which is likely the reason the name garnered such notoriety after *Sins* and the sex scandals.¶ However, the role his infamy plays in *Letters* is decidedly less apparent. While the character he plays in *Sins*, Eveline, is a key part of the narrative in *Letters*, the connection to Saul's supposed real life is all but non-existent. It is up to readers to remind

---

* See Appendix for examples.
† *Sins*, p. 36.
‡ See Hyde, *The Cleveland Street Scandal*.
§ See Morris Kaplan, *Sodom on the Thames*, p. 203.
¶ For more on Saul, see the introduction to *Sins* (2013).

themselves of the connection, though this adds little while reading
the text. *Letters* is touted as an 'appendix' to *Sins* even though the
text barely acknowledges its predecessor. As with the conjecture
on the publication provenance of the 1903 edition of *Letters* which
I will discuss below, we can similarly speculate on the reasons for
the production of the text in the first place.

It was not an uncommon practice for pornographic texts in the
Victorian period to reference or be based on previous works. Some
texts, such as *Letters* which carried a price of over £6, were available to a limited audience with the means to procure them, while
others were sold more cheaply and available to a wider audience.
Nevertheless, it is likely that many texts were known to collectors.
If we assume a certain level of knowledge to those consuming
the works in question, it would not be a great leap to claim that
the mention of *Sins* and characters from it in an advertisement
for pornographic texts would be enough to capture the attention,
desire, and, most importantly, money of potential readers. The
most accessible example of this practice is the use of Oscar Wilde's
name in various forgeries printed in the early twentieth century
most famously by publisher Leonard Smithers.* Scandalousness
was a powerful sales tool, much as it is today.

Plot of *Letters from Laura and Eveline*

Letters purports to be an appendix of *The Sins of the Cities of
the Plain*, though the two share little similarity. *Sins* is presented
as a memoir of its protagonist, Jack Saul, which allegedly docu-
ments life in London's underground sex trade (even if they are a
bit tongue-in-cheek, as Wolfram Setz has pointed out in his introduction to the text).† *Letters* sets up a similar style of narrative yet
the resulting text amounts to repetitive descriptions of sex acts
between 'husbands', 'wives', and others at Inslip's Club and aboard
a steamship. This repetition is the very thing that Mr. Cambon,
the wealthy patron of Jack Saul who commissions his memoirs

---

* See James G. Nelson, *Publisher to the Decadents* (2000).
† See *Sins* pp. v-xxv (2013).

in *Sins*, does not wish to "pall upon"* his readers. So, as we see in *Sins*, the narrative as told through Saul's printed memoirs is a series of events which track his progression sexually and showcases the fluidity of Victorian ideas about sexuality, in that he has encounters with men and women in almost equal amounts. *Letters* touches on this fluidity in that its protagonists fantasize that they are hermaphrodites, though it is portrayed as more or less a kink or fantasy rather than a self-aware expression of sexualities.

In a sense, *Letters* feels like a mockery of the pornographic genre. From the outset the reader is informed that the story told is of a mock-marriage and, if we are using *Sins* as our guide, all the participants are well aware of Laura's and Eveline's genders; that is, everyone knows they are males dressed in female clothing. The fantasy in *Letters* is that Laura and Eveline are hermaphrodites though their husbands act as if they are biologically females with enlarged clitorises that are wielded and treated just like penises, with all the repeating references to Priapus, semen (spendings), and hyperbolic language in reference to the immense size of the members being described.

Letters fits into the pornography of the day by way of its lecherous descriptions of sexual acts, though it tends towards a style that can only be described as bordering on the absurd. While many of the expected pornographic tropes are present—the taking of maidenheads, rape victim turned nymphomaniac, massive penises ejaculating massive amounts of semen—something seems amiss in *Letters*. While pornography is seldom treated as great literary work, oftentimes there can be redeeming qualities in terms of how the text fits within or follows its genre's established frameworks. *Letters*, Ashbee's chastisement notwithstanding, acts very much like a 'standard' pornographic work but goes further in exploding the expectations that come with following the 'rules'. It contains the expected paternalistic hierarchy and misogyny present in much pornography, but given the gender reversals in *Letters* and the subversion of heterocentric traditions (marriage, for example) there is

---

* *Sins*, p. 10.

much more happening below the surface than in the average work of pornographic fiction. What may seem like a poorly-crafted work intended only to make its publisher money appears, in fact, to be a mockery of the trade as well as strictly-defined sexualities and that in itself has literary value and merits further study.

Provenance of the Text for This Edition

The text of this edition of *Letters from Laura and Eveline* is based on a 1903 reprint of the 1883 original.* The 1883 edition appears not to have survived though Ashbee, whose massive collection of pornographic and erotic works was donated to the British Library upon his death in 1900, describes the original as a "serial with the volume to which it forms a sequel [*The Sins of the Cities of the Plain*]; pp. 77; two lines on title-page; 'issue limited to fifty copies'; price £6 6s" (402). In addition, Ashbee claims that the text is "from the pen of its publisher" (403), William Lazenby, one of the major producers of pornographic texts in London between 1873-1886. The present edition is taken not from Lazenby's initial printing, but a later Parisian reprint on account of the first edition being lost. Lazenby, who sometimes worked under the alias Duncan Cameron,† was responsible for publishing a number of pornographic 'classics' such as *The Romance of Lust* (ca. 1873), periodicals *The Pearl* (1879-1880) and *The Cremorne* (1882), *The Sins of the Cities of the Plain* (1881), and of course *Letters from Laura and Eveline* (1883). He is even, as Ashbee has suggested, thought to have been the writer of a good deal of the work he published.

The 1903 printing upon which this edition is based represents the third known printing of the original work. The first, of course, is the original 1883 printing by William Lazenby that Ashbee discusses. A second edition was printed in Paris in 1899 by a printer

---

* I am grateful to the British Library for providing a microfilm copy of the 1903 edition (P.C.13c.11). I am also grateful to the University of British Columbia Library for obtaining it on my behalf. See Mendes, *Clandestine Erotic Fiction in English 1800-1930*, pp. 350-351.

† See Peter Mendes, *Clandestine Fiction in English 1800-1930*, pp. 4-5.

called Renaudie for the French bookseller Charles Hirsch. Hirsch is perhaps best known as the bookseller who claimed his London bookshop, the *Librarie Parisienne*, was used by Oscar Wilde and a group of other writers as a drop off point in the round robin production of the homosexual romance novel *Teleny* (1893). Hirsch's story and Wilde's hand in the book's production have never been verified, of course.* The third edition of *Letters* (1903), which the present edition uses as its source, was also produced by Hirsch in the same manner as the 1899 edition. Since the 1903 edition is the only one known to have survived, we have to treat it as extant and there is no cause to think that that the editions varied greatly.†

The reasons for reprinting *Letters* are subject to conjecture as well. Because there is no known reprint of *Sins*—which acts as the first in the series, if we can call it that—by this group, it is difficult to make the argument that *Letters* was re-released as part of a set the way modern series are sometimes packaged and sold. Though there is no known reprint of *Sins* that coincides with the 1903 reprint of *Letters*, this does not mean that there was not one that simply did not survive. What we do know is that the closest surviving reprint of *Sins* was a 1902 edition for the Erotica Biblion Society of London and New York. It is also difficult to determine which publishers collaborated with each other and Hirsch could have had a hand in publishing the 1902 reprint of *Sins* or an unknown companion to his 1903 edition of *Letters*. Regardless of the editions that were or were not released, a more practical reason likely occasioned Hirsch's reprint of *Letters* or any work: money. There is every reason to think Hirsch would have rushed a new edition out if he felt it would make him money. He was, after all, in the business of selling books. A rushed printing—not to mention the printing in a French-speaking country—may account for the many printing errors that have been corrected in this edition but preserved in the appendix.

JUSTIN O'HEARN
University of British Columbia

* See Hirsch's "Notice" in *Teleny* (Valancourt, 2010) p. 171.
† See Mendes, *Clandestine*, p. 350.

Notes on the Corrected Text of *Letters from Laura and Eveline*

The source text for *Letters from Laura and Eveline* is, as stated in the introduction, a facsimile of the 1903 edition. That edition contains numerous errors due to the nature of its seemingly hasty publication by Charles Hirsch. I have corrected these errors to afford a smoother reading experience. However, the errors in typography and spelling are part of texts such as this and give further insight into the contexts of their production. We can only speculate as to how each error occurred in reality, but it may be surmised that the intended audience was powerless to demand higher quality editions and simply overlooked or accepted the errors and poor quality as part of the overall experience of books such as this. A full list of corrections can be found in the appendix at the back of this volume for those interested. Also in the appendix are contextual materials about the Boulton and Park case, including the correspondence alluded to in the introduction above and the text of a penny pamphlet about the trial itself.

A few spelling variations of note that may not be familiar to the modern reader require explanation. 'Arse-quim' also appears as 'arsequim' throughout the original text. Other variants of this word are 'arse-vagina', 'arse-cunt', and the more sterile 'rectum vagina'. There are multiple instances of the word 'extatic' which is a variant spelling of 'ecstatic'. I have not changed these instances. While this spelling was not common in the Victorian period, it may be a spectre of the text's overseas printing. Elsewhere, however, 'ecstasy' appears spelled correctly.

I have also preserved various anomalies in capitalization. This is most apparent in instances of dialogue especially after exclamation points. In the source text, sometimes the word—usually an interjection—after an exclamation point is capitalized but, more often than not, it is not.

The variant spelling of 'pussy' as 'pussey' may look odd to most modern readers, but this was an accepted spelling in the period. As with 'pussy/pussey', the Victorians also accepted 'dildo' and 'dildoe', both of which appear in the present volume unaltered.

Bibliography and Further Reading

Ashbee, Henry Spencer. 1885. *Bibliography of Prohibited Books*. 3 vols. New York: Jack Brussel, 1962.

Cook, Matt. *London and the Culture of Homosexuality, 1885-1914*. Cambridge: Cambridge University Press, 2003.

Hyde, H. Montgomery. *The Other Love: An Historical and Contemporary Survey of Homosexuality in Britain*. London: Heinemann, 1970.

——. *The Cleveland Street Scandal*. London: W. H. Allen, 1976.

Kaplan, Morris B. *Sodom on the Thames: Sex, Love, and Scandal in Wilde Times*. Ithaca: Cornell University Press, 2005.

Kearney, Patrick J. *The Private Case: An Annotated Bibliography of the Private Case Erotica Collection in the British (Museum) Library*. London: J. Landesman, 1981.

——. *A History of Erotic Literature*. London: Macmillan, 1982.

Koven, Seth. *Slumming: Sexual and Social Politics in Victorian London*. Princeton: Princeton University Press, 2006.

Mackie, Gregory. "Publishing Notoriety: Piracy, Pornography, and Oscar Wilde." *University of Toronto Quarterly* 73.4 (2004): 980.

Marcus, Steven. *The Other Victorians: A Study of Sexuality and Pornography in Mid-Nineteenth-Century England*. New York: Basic Books, 1966.

Mendes, Peter. *Clandestine Erotic Fiction in English, 1800-1930: A Bibliographical Study*. Aldershot, England: Ashgate Publishing, 1998.

The Sins of the Cities of the Plain. 1881. Kansas City: Valancourt Books, 2012.

Teleny, or, The Reverse of the Medal. 1893. Kansas City: Valancourt Books, 2010.

LETTERS

FROM

Laura and Eveline

GIVING AN ACCOUNT OF THEIR

Mock=Marriage, Wedding Trip

ETC.

PUBLISHED AS AN

APPENDIX TO THE SINS OF THE CITIES

LONDON
PRIVATELY PRINTED
1903

LETTER

FROM

LAURA TO LOUIS H——

DEAREST LOUIS,

At length I am a bride; Lord Arthur was so pathetic, and appealed to earnestly to every sentiment of my love, that I could not do otherwise than entrust my happiness to his keeping, and agree to a speedy marriage; so rather more than a week ago we were made man and wife, consummated our nuptials, took a short six days' tour, then back to town, where last night Inslip's Club gave a grand but very select ball in our honour, and to celebrate the auspicious event.

I must also tell you that dear Eveline was married at the same time to that huge Guardsman, Lord Rasper, and as I am going to let you into all our private affairs, you will find that happy pair pretty considerably mixed up with our doings.

I need scarcely tell you how the thoughts of becoming a bride fluttered my virgin heart, only to think of being naked in bed with a fine fellow like Arthur, who I only too truly guessed would be most formidably armed with a Cupid's spear, commensurate with the very ominous bunch in his trousers, which always had a peculiar fascination to me. How glad I was not to be kept very long in suspense; he proposed on Sunday, and we fixed Wednesday for the event of our lives.

Archdeacon Vaseline undertook to perform the ceremony, by special license, at Inslip's Club, which was fitted up as a

chapel for the occasion, the windows being all darkened and
Count R—— lent them his splendid silver-gilt candlesticks,
each one of which represented the emblem of our worship
a huge priapus, set straight up as we like to see them in life,
the bases being composed of finely-moulded testicles, beautifully carved so that the representation of balls, hair, &c.,
was most lifelike.

They burnt an aphrodisiacal incense in a curious kind of
lamp, made of opal and pink-coloured glass, in the shape of
arse-cunts.

There were twelve of them on the altar table, the rest of
the chapel, which was a veritable shrine of voluptuousness
being brilliantly lighted up by the usual chandeliers and can-
delabra, the mirrors round the walls reflecting the gay and
festive party.

This does not appear to have been the first wedding that
has taken place there, as Inslip had all the necessary furni-
ture on hand, the altar being profusely decorated with
flowers, and surmounted by a large marble life-size copy
of the "Venus Callypyge," that is "Venus of the beautiful
arse,"* showing the object of adoration at Inslip's, set off by
two beautifully-carved effigies of Priapus,† with monstrous
pricks, each pointing to the exquisite buttocks of the Venus,
whilst the white silken altar cloth had embroidered groups
of voluptuous sodomy in each corner. The altar piece was a
magnificent painting of subjects exquisitely designed after the
ideas of the Marquis de Sade, in "Justine and Juliette" and "La
Philosophie dans le Boudoir", showing every possible kind of

* An ancient Roman statue, whose name literally means 'Venus of the beautiful
buttocks', thought to be a copy of an older Greek statue called Aphrodite
Kallipygos.
† Priapus is a Greco-Roman god of procreation and fertility whose effigies are
usually of a deformed figure with a large penis. The term Priapus, and its variants,
is often used simply as slang for penis.

sodomite enjoyment, and in addition to this masterpiece of the painter's art, every available space between the mirrors on the walls was occupied by some artistic representation of pederastic* voluptuousness, showing every conceivable fancy or whim so delicious to votaries of sodomite whorship.[1]

Count R—— gave us away, and the two groomsmen were Captain Bull and General Wilkes, who have only recently joined the club; there were sixteen bridesmaids and fifteen other gentlemen[2] besides the Archdeacon.

Both Eveline and myself were in a perfect trepidation of excitement all the previous day, and we were careful to occupy separate rooms at night for fear that our feelings should lead us into some indiscretions, and render us not quite so fit as we required to be to properly sustain[3] our parts next day.†

Talking of parts, how my prick fairly stood and throbbed with emotion, as my thoughts anticipated all that was likely to occur, and during a short visit to Inslip's in the course of the day I inspected the two bridal chambers where the marriages were to be consummated, pressed my hands on the soft springy beds, admired the lovely lace trimmings to the curtains, the light-blue silk coverlets, the toilet services, &c.; and I may mention that the "lady's" pot de chambre had a glorious prick painted inside it, whilst that of the bridegroom was ornamented by a deliciously painted arse-quim,‡ slightly

---

* It should be noted that 'pederasty' in the Victorian period did not necessarily imply sex with children. It usually connoted sex between older and younger men (teenagers or men in their early twenties).

† This may be a reference to *Sins* pp. 45-52 in which Eveline and Laura (and Selina) enjoy each other's sexual company after a ball at Inslip's.

‡ It is unclear, at times, precisely what 'arse-quim' refers to. While it is clear to readers that Laura is a hermaphrodite it is not as clear that her bridegroom is aware and it would therefore be strange for him to see an 'arse-quim' rather than simply a 'quim' ornamenting his chamber pot. As the title of the work suggests that theirs is a 'mock marriage', however, it might indicate that the bridegroom is in on the secret.

open, so as to look more like a throbbing rose-bud than any-thing.

Then knowing my bridegroom to be very full of curiosity as to the doings of others, I looked to see if there were any peep-holes for us to spy the actions of Lord Rasper and his bride when they retired like ourselves to consummate their nuptials. Mr. Inslip, who was showing me the arrangements, soon put me up to the trick of little pieces in the door of communication between the two rooms, could be noise-lessly slipped out, so as to give a first-rate view of every thing in the next apartment.*

Eveline and myself were both to be dressed alike, and it took us nearly till eight o'clock in the evening before we were ready to be led to the altar by Count K——. No one would have known us from lovely girls of seventeen or eighteen, as we surveyed ourselves in the cheval-glass. Our dresses were superb white satin, trimmed with Valenciennes lace, and Honiton lace veils; we had also coronets of pearls and diamonds, with earrings, necklaces and bracelets to match. For myself I can always command sufficient colour to dis-pense with rouge or cosmetics, and Eveline's was an equally genuine complexion. It is scarcely necessary to mention our under-clothing, but there was everything to excite desire in our husbands as they would go through the delicious cer-emony of taking off our things preparatory to taking our virginities between the sheets; pretty tight-laced corsets reducing our waists to fourteen or[4] fifteen inches, which made the shape of our large arses ravishingly suggestive, as they struck out voluptuously behind; we had flesh-coloured dress improvers, or false bubbies, made of the most delicate kid leather, so that they were as like the real things as possible,

---

* Eveline watches Laura and Arthur through a peephole in *Sins*, p. 38

they fitted so nicely, and were delicately set off[5] by the rich lace of our chemises, beneath this upper stratum, as I might call it, were our drawers, which, of course, took in the tails of our chemises, tucked most provokingly over our fannies[6] and fitting so tightly as almost to defy the inquisitive searcher who might try to find the opening in front, or for that matter behind either, so beautifully were our caleçons made to fit the coutour of our persons, whilst the thighs down to the knee were so closely encased that they clearly indicated the upward swell to the hips, without the least embarrassing wrinkle to spoil the tout-ensemble which was finished off by a lovely lace fringe just below the knee, so as to set off to perfection as pretty pairs of legs as you could possibly find on any two ladies in London, although speaking of myself I really am proud of my understandings, especially when set off by such white silk stockings and pretty chaussures* as we were fitted with.

My bridesmaids were eight dark beauties dressed in ivory silk, trimmed with ruby velvet large Rubens hats with long drooping ruby feathers.

Eveline had eight fair virgins for her attendants to the altar, in pale mauve silk with square bodices and elbow sleeves, Marie Stuart bonnets of white tulle, large pearls round the front and sprays of apple blossom falling over the hair at the back; long kid gloves of pale lemon colour and white satin boots completed their costumes.

I need not worry you by writing all the details of the ceremony in the church, which had an enormous priapus in the shape of a reading desk with a sounding board in the

* *Caleçons*: Male underwear, usually translated as 'boxers' now. *Coutour*: possibly a misspelling of 'contour' or the French word 'couture', which would also make some sense considering the context and the other French terms in this passage. *Tout-ensemble*: the whole outfit. *Chaussures*: a general term for anything worn on the feet.

fashion of a lovely arse-cunt, the underpart over the reader's head being painted and carved to represent that voluptuous organ of love. Priapi abounded in every decoration,[7] even the pipes of the organ were fashioned like pricks. The Venerable Archdeacon, as we approached the altar stood up with his book in his hand, whilst a youthful acolyte kneeling before him, parted his loose robe of white lawn (which was ornamented all over by embroidery representing the emblem of love in designs of gold and crimson needlework), and taking his standing prick in hand, gently frigged as the service proceeded, and managed so adroitly that at the words—"With this ring I thee wed, with my body I thee worship, &c.," he spent right in my face, even favouring Eveline with a few drops, which made us blush up to our eyes, and happening to glance round[8] I observed the two groomsmen, Capt. Bull[9] and General Wilkes, were slyly handling each other's pricks almost under the eyes of the bridesmaids. At length they conducted us to the bridesmaids. At length they conducted us to the vestry,[10] where the register was signed and witnessed; then all sat down in the banqueting-hall to a sumptuous wedding breakfast,* the organ playing a wedding march.

Count R—— took the head of the table, having us newly-married couples on his right and left.

Lord Arthur's prick was so rampant that, letting it out of its confinement, I had to keep my left hand on it under the table, and noticed that every gentleman[11] had a bridesmaid or lady similarly attentive to them.

It was a curious sight to watch the emotions depicted on the various faces as they felt themselves being worked up to an extatic crisis; but Eveline and myself having more serious business in prospect, did not push things to the spending

---

* It was customary to have weddings at an early hour in Victorian England and thus the reception meal would be a breakfast.

point, but quietly awaited our chance, after the usual healths had been honoured, to slip away to our respective rooms, where we had to wait a[12] little while before the advent of our anxiously expected spouses as they could leave the table to join us.

How my heart beat, and my virgin arse throbbed, and[13] my stiff prick stood in anticipation of expected delights.

Rat-a-tat-tat softly at the door soon announced Arthur to my ready ears, yet I did not respond in a moment; just then I was indulging in a very curious kind of[14] voluptuous reverie, sitting in a low easy lounging chair, fancying Arthur was already undressing me with his own clothes all off except his shirt, which was sticking out quite a quarter of a yard in front, as his great fine cock[15] stood proudly erect. He tapped at the door again, whispering—"Lady Laura! Laura, dearest; are you asleep? May I come in?"

Springing up I ran eagerly to the door clasping my arms around his darling neck as he entered, and responding with all my ardour to his hot burning kisses.

"What a time you have been, Arthur. I thought you would never come, my darling. Surely you love your little Laura better than a glass or two of wine, my sweet?"

"You shall find me come quick enough, my lady, when once I have got you in bed. Let me help you, dearest love, to undress?"

"For shame, Arthur dear; how can you be so rude! oh! let me put out the lights first!" as he was already beginning to put his hand up my clothes.

"You may well say shame, Laura, do you think I would be cheated like that of my first sight of all your ladyship's[16] naked blushing charms; how could I enjoy the confusion you will be in presently when my rude hand takes little liberties? those first touches, and the sight of your shy coyness are, or rather will be, such inconceivably exquisite pleasures, I would not miss the sight of it for the world. In the dark, indeed, none but stupid mock modest fools shun a brilliant light on their love, and I have sworn to have your maidenhead in your bridal dress."

Blushing scarlet and palpitating with emotion at being treated exactly like a woman, a delicious sensation thrilled through my veins, and my arse-quim throbbed again like a true cunt.

His nervous hands were now busy as he impetuously threw me on the bed, all as I was in my bridal costume. I felt his hot touches already on my thighs, which were nervously crossed to resist his rudeness.

"I will see and kiss your lovely fanny, Laura; it's no use shutting your legs like that, now you are my wife," he exclaimed, his face colouring and his eyes almost flashing fire, so tremendously excited was he.

I was afraid to look at him, and hid my crimson face in a pillow which I pulled over it. My legs relaxed their tightness a little, and his hand was forced between my thighs, he found the slit in my drawers, and tossing up white satin dress and skirts to my waist, ruthlessly pulled aside the tail of my chemise which yet protected my poor throbbing virginity.

"My God, love! oh, Laura, what a splendid clitoris you have. You are like an hermaphrodite; it's[17] quite as long as my prick. Is it always excited and stiff like this? Oh! oh; let me kiss it darling? Will it spend, dearest Laura? Oh, what a voluptuous darling treasure you are!"

Still hiding my face and ready to faint with shame, I yet felt how delicious it was to be handled and touched by the man I loved so much, and fancied myself a girl or a real hermaphrodite, and my prick only a big clitoris; how my arse thrilled with hot lust, and pouted just like a cunt.

"What a lovely morsel!" he ejaculated, kissing it up and down its whole length, and finishing by taking the ruby head between his eager lips, and sucking me voluptuously, whilst at the same time I felt one of his hands slipping underneath between the division of my thighs, and groping till a finger began to postillion* my quivering arse-cunt. My sensations at that moment were simply quite inexpressible, with one great throb of excitement (my feelings had been so long suppressed), I boiled over, and his amorous mouth was simply inundated by a perfect flood of spendings; how eagerly he sucked and swallowed all to the uttermost drop of the creamy[18] juice, whilst his finger probed and almost drove me wild with lustful desire by its searching insertions[19] in my raging behind.

Instinctively my hands pressed lovingly on his head to keep him where he was, and if possible force myself further into his mouth.

He had been leaning over the bed, but now springing up behind me, made me kneel up with my face in the pillow, throwing my bridal dress over my back, quite regardless of the damage to my veil, orange wreath, &c., as he pulled open my drawers as wide as possible behind, so that he could feast his eyes on the splendid expanse of my fat white alabaster buttocks, which seemed to have an indescribable fascination to him.

"My God, I can't wait, after the restraint I've had to put on myself all day!" he exclaimed, glueing his lips to the pouting throbbing orifice of my arsequim, as his hands held apart the cheeks of my splendid bottom, the touches of his tongue so increased the burning heat of those parts that I writhed from the intensity of my desires and hot lust.

---

* This is an archaic term for a courier or post-boy. While its use as a verb is odd, it is interesting nonetheless for its subtle allusion to Victorian post-boys who were known to moonlight as rent-boys.

Just then, peeping out a little, my eyes caught sight of his tremendous weapon,[20] I should say quite a foot long, and as big round as a lady's wrist, eight inches round at least, the skin drawn back, the dark coloured ruby head was distended by the rush of blood to the parts, which I have read is the cause of the manly stiffness, when they are excited; his bollocks were enormously swollen, full of boiling spunk.*

"There, Laura, darling, look at the dear thing which is to consummate our happiness, and remove your irksome virginity; don't be afraid of its size, although[21] big and tremendously hard when he stands like this in his glory, no small tender hole ever yet was so tight that he could not get in, and give pleasure, too, my lovely darling. The little pain at first is nothing, to the heavenly bliss you will feel[22] afterwards; but I burn with hot desire. Do tell me you will love me, and help all my efforts to effect the consummation of our mutual desires. Oh, Laura, darling, why do you hide your face in the pillow, why don't you speak, and tell me you love me?"

Shivering with emotion it was yet so awfully delicious to be taken for a woman, and addressed as a woman, his manly caresses and terms of endearment, really added to my blushing bashfulness, at the same time perfectly irresistible thrills of desire pervaded[23] my person, which seemed to concentrate in my longing arse-quim. What extatic delights must such a prick as I had caught a glance of be capable of giving! I turned up my face to his as he was bending over me, and again throwing my arms round his dear neck, glued my mouth to his warm lips, still rich and luscious from my aromatic spendings, the slightly pungent flavour of which

---

* The *OED* has the earliest usage for 'spunk' listed as c.1890 in the erotic memoir *My Secret Life*. The present text's use of the word would predate this by seven years, its initial publication being 1883. Unfortunately, this cannot be verified, as the source of the present text was the 1903 reprint.

yet hung about them as he returned my kisses, thrusting his slippery tongue between[24] my teeth till its velvet tip revelled and played inside my mouth in such soul-stirring touches, that I drew deep sighs of desire, as I murmured—.

"Arthur, dearest, you won't hurt your little Laura, will you, my love? Oh! for heaven's sake be gentle, if you find me rather too small for that dreadful looking monster I just saw. Oh, love, I do indeed want to make you happy, and submit person, everything to your love. You may kill me if you like, I love you so dearly."

He seemed quite touched by my deep emotion, tenderly caressing my slightly upturned bottom again.

"Laura, dear," he whispered, "your darling arsequim is so far below, or rather behind, that I think your present position is the most favourable one for our business, especially darling, if you will turn up your lovely bottom a little more."

"More on your knees, darling, and your legs wide open," he whispered again. "Don't scream, if you can help it, or Rasper and Eveline will be hearing and laugh at us."

I shifted a little, and at the same time he undid the waistband of my drawers, pulling them down altogether, thus exposing all my big arse to his view, which he kissed rapturously as he stretched across the bed behind me, and I could feel his face again right in the crack of my buttocks, his tongue tickling, and his warm breath and beard and moustache titillating[25] to madness the tight little twitching hole he was about to ravish by storm, whilst his hands deliciously fingered and played with what he called my glorious clitoris, which was now quite slippery with a fresh emission, which his touches brought down again.

My emotions were so excessive, that I almost gasped for breath, and scarcely knew what he was doing till I felt the head of his tremendous hot prick pressing for admission

behind. He had wetted it with his saliva, and notwithstanding the tightness of my sphincter muscle[26], the head of his
affair at once got in about an inch, and there stuck, as it were,
by his[27] shoulders, in spite of his hard shoves.

"My God, you will kill me Arthur, dear. Oh! I can't bear it,
indeed I can't," the intense pain forced me to groan out.

Just then I felt quite a warm gush of his sperm shoot into
my bottom, and I pushed out my arse as an acknowledge-
ment of his tribute, just as he plunged on to take advantage
of the easing his spending was likely to afford; but he gained
very little ground, and the stretching, tearing pain was so
awful I screamed—"Ah! ah! Oh! oh! oh! You'll kill me," and
actually fainted under it.

Presently I returned to my senses, and found he had
somehow made a considerable advance, as I could certainly
feel[28] his insertion of four or five inches; he had twisted my
face round so as to kiss and tip me the velvet tip of his dear
tongue. My bottom felt awfully gorged and stretched, yet
with most voluptuous sensations, and one of his hands had
my cock-clitoris deliciously grasped, frigging me beautifully,
and giving such pleasure, that it very considerably soothed
my pains.

"Push on, now, Arthur, dear; make me a woman at once.
This pain is so awful, yet I feel a lovely thrill in my veins, and
such excitement, both in my bottom and in front, where you
play with me so nicely that I feel I must have you, if I die for
it. Oh! my God, shove it up if you split me!"

"Now, love, meet me for the last push!" he replied, grinding his teeth with erotic passion and lust. "For God's sake let
me get in, or I shall go quite mad. I will fuck you, if I kill you,
and smash you to atoms!"

Drawing my breath, and pushing out my bottom, and
heaving backwards the first agonizing stroke achieved a

further advance as I screamed with agony, but the next quite demolished further resistance, and left his fine prick, after a hard fought assault in full possession of my arse-quim, its utmost length throbbing in my tightly-fitting hot sheath, now rendered far more comfortable by our profuse spendings which the sheets afterwards amply testified were tinged with blood.

Now commenced a really luscious and voluptuous bottom fucking; moving gently at first, he so increased the speed of his stroke that I was fairly delirious from excessive emotions, both of us seemed to swim in a bath of continual spendings, again and again did the seminal elixir of love spurt from us in streams, till at last we sank flat, quite enervated on the bed, as I enjoyed the luscious sensations his still stiff and throbbing machine caused as he kept it still in my arse, which clasped his darling prick like a true vagina; after soaking for many minutes in a state of sweet delirium he withdrew his still half standing prick with a great plop.

"Now darling," he exclaimed, giving my arse a shower of kisses, "whatever you were before, you have lost your virginity, and are my blooming arsefucking wife for ever." He then tore off my bridal veil and orange blossoms.

"And I'm your wife, my dearest husband, I'm lady Arthur C——. You dear man, I could[29] die in your strong embrace, and give up my soul in ecstasy under the strokes of your glorious prick!" I sighed in reply, having hardly yet recovered from the delicious excitement.

After a little toying together, "Arthur," said I, covering him with kisses, "darling, would you like to peep at them in the other room; yesterday I found out some spying holes in the door when I came to look over the rooms?"

"Yes, love," giving me repeated kisses, "what a darling you are, and what exquisite pleasure taking your virginity has afforded me. I am very curious to see how they get on, for Rasper is the joke in the Guards for his enormous cock. Let us refresh our parts in cold water, then we shall be ready to renew our joys if the sight of them makes us excited, as no doubt it will."

Presently, after a glass of champagne, I quietly slipped out the pieces from the door, and found our friends had not made such progress as we had. Eveline had still got her bridal dress on, so they had evidently been wasting their time spooning each other, and we saw Rasper throw off his coat, but his bride seemed very slow in following his example. She was sitting in a lounging chair, with veil and orange blossoms still on.

"Come, dear," said Lord Rasper, "it's[30] time we began business now. Lord Arthur will have done for Laura by this."

Eveline put her hands to her face, which was suffused with blushes, and sobbed—.

"Oh no! wait till another time; you're such a dreadful big made man, you will split me in two, and I'm so afraid,[31] as one of the bridesmaids told me jokingly—"

Here she stopped, and Rasper firing up with passion exclaimed—

"Which little bitch was it? Damn it, she's heard the regimental chaff. Eveline, my prick shall split you without mercy, if you don't tell me at once what she said."

"My darling love oh, Rasper, forgive me for saying so, but she did say you were hung like a stallion! Oh, my! I can never have any thing to do with you, dear,"[32] replied Eveline, very much frightened.

"We'll see about that, my darling; trust to me and you won't be too much hurt. Is its[33] little pussey cat afraid I shall split it? Let me feel if it is too much scared!" he said, falling[34] on one knee before her, and putting his right hand up her clothes.

"What lovely legs you have, dearest, and tightfitting drawers, and such soft, velvety[35] thighs. Ha! I've found its[36] trembling pussey cat. My love, what a lovely clitoris, and stiff with love; it shan't be hurt, the little darling, let me kiss it and[37] comfort it a little."

Saying which he raised her clothes quite up to her waist, and we could see his hand held as fine a prick as any young fellow could wish to be blessed with; he had only opened Eveline's drawers a little in front, so that the appendages were not visible, only some lovely light auburn hair, and we had a splendid view of the close-fitting lawn drawers which encased her thighs, finishing in a fringe of lace just below the knee, one leg of the drawers being tucked up where his groping hand had felt her thighs, giving a most suggestive view of a little delicate white flesh, a contrast to the rose-coloured stockings below, which were set off by lovely blue silk garters (at least we could see one). To crown all Eveline had most ravishingly small feet, in white satin shoes.

Rasper had let out his enormous muscular cock, which was at least two inches longer than my husband's and even thicker, that is over thirteen inches long and nine inches round; this, lifting one of her feet, he made her caress with her foot, rubbing the soft sole of her new satin shoes over his big prick, so as to gently roll it on his thigh, and churning up his full bollocks.

Then keeping up the delightful illusion as to her being a woman, he went on to kiss and fondle Eveline's cock, calling it "a darling love of a clitoris," &c., fit for any hermaphrodite.[38]

At first he tickled its ruby head with the tip of his tongue, then taking it into his mouth, sucked with great gusto till his inamorata* fairly writhed and twisted about in her chair,

---

* A female lover.

and we guessed she was spending as we could see some of the creamy drops glistening on his moustache as they had overflowed from his mouth, and presently also the delicious rolling of her soft boot on his prick made it spout out a perfect stream of love juice, and both of them seemed for a minute or so quite oblivious of everything, so carried away had they been by their excessive emotions.

Presently he rose from his knees, and kissing her passionately, exclaimed—

"Oh, Eveline, you are a darling, that clitoris of yours doubles my love for you; how I shall kiss and pet it always. But now, dearest, I really think it is time we tried to effect the conjunction of love, so as to carry out the injunction in the marriage ceremony of procreating children, &c., so as to keep the earth replenished. My sweet love, let us hope that every girl may have such a clitoris as you have, and every boy a prick like mine, so as to be worthy of their parents, who got them."

"I'm so impatient for your maidenhead" he went on, "I must fuck your lovely arse-cunt* this very moment; kissing your clitoris has given me such a horn nothing but that can relieve. Look, dearest, take it in your hand, the delicious foot-frigging you treated it to just now has but made me worse!"

He had now got[39] her standing against the side of the bed, as he placed his prick in her hand. We could see her crimson all over face and neck in blushing confusion; though covered by her wedding veil, his hands were again under her dress, caressing her fine cock-clitoris of Eveline's[40] and groping her arse-quim behind.

"Oh, let me undress, and put out the lights, dear. Oh, do; there's a love; I'm so afraid, and so ashamed!" she said, appealingly.

---

* This seems at odds with the sentiment Lord Rasper just finished, namely, that he wants to impregnate Eveline.

"No, no!" he replied, almost fiercely. "I can't wait now; damn the damage! I mean to have you just as you are, get on the bed and kneel up."

He was so strong and impetuous, that without waiting for Eveline to comply with his request, he fairly tossed her on the bed, in all her bridal paraphernalia of orange blossoms, lace and white satin, &c. He was up behind her in a second, throwing her dress and satin petticoats well over her back, we had a lovely view of her plump white buttocks, encased in tight fitting drawers; these he tore open as widely as possible, showing[41] the dazzling whiteness of her fair, fat, plump, charms.

"Ah! ah! Oh, do be gentle!" she sobbed. "You'll hurt me so, I am sure. Oh! oh!"[42] as he commenced to explore all the beauties of her palpitating wrinkled, rosy, and pouting tight arse-cunt.

Just wetting the head of his tremendous prick, which to me was really awful to contemplate, he brought its ruby swollen top to the mark, and pushed as it seemed very viciously to get into his victim, making poor Eveline fairly scream with pain.

"You must bear it, darling; have courage; I shall get in presently, then all your pain will be turned to pleasure," he said, grinding his teeth, and holding her buttocks with a grip of iron, as he ruthlessly pushed his enormous prick at her quivering, throbbing arse-cunt.

"Ah—r—r—re," screamed his bride, in a long drawn agony, as he appeared to us to be getting in slightly; such a fierce delight seemed to sparkle in his eyes, whilst his face flushed with passion.

"Scream away; it's delightful to hear it. I will fuck you now if I kill you! Ask me to fuck you, you darling. Isn't that a nice word; it comprehends all the delights of sex in one short expressive word. Oh! how I will fuck you!"

His efforts seemed fruitless; the head of his tremendous machine seemed fairly in an inch or so, and there stuck fast by some obstruction. Poor Eveline had hidden her face in the pillow, groaning and sobbing[43] with pain and shame, her veil over her face.

Her husband waiting a minute or so to get his breath, and recover from spending again, rammed into her, exclaiming—

"Now, or never, my darling; my spunk will have eased you a bit; shove out your splendid arse, and ask me to fuck you well."

"Oh, Rasper, my love, make haste and do it now, if I die. Oh! fuck—fuck—fuck me, dearest husband till you make a woman of your Eveline. Ah! Ah!—r—re—. Ah! Oh, my god! Oh! oh! oh!"

"I can't bear it," she exclaimed, in intense agony, wriggling her arse so as quite[44] to throw his prick out of position, and we could see its ruddy head all glistening with spendings and slightly blood-stained.

After a slight pause he[45] re-adjusted it to the point of attack, but another thought seemed to strike him, and he recommenced kissing her delicious arse-quim, whilst his hands slipping around to her front, where evidently frigging the fine erect clitoris he was so rapturously fond of.

Having a rather oblique view, we could see everything even his tongue minetting* her twitching, rosy bottom-hole.

This so excited Lord Arthur that he would have carried me again to the bed, had I not begged him to restrain himself and let me watch the voluptuous sight of Rasper and his bride.

"I'll pet, and gently frig your prick," I whispered, taking

---

* This is a bit of obscure Victorian erotic slang no longer in use. 'Minette' comes from the feminine form of the French 'minet' which is a diminutive for cat, similar to 'kitty' or 'pussy'. In this context, however, it is obviously a term for cunnilingus or, in this case, anilingus masquerading as cunnilingus for the purposes of fantasy.

it in hand, and throwing my arm lovingly round his waist,
which caresses he repaid by getting his middle finger in my
arse-vagina, and, postillioning me exquisitely.

But to return to our mutton*—as the French say—Rasper
was now putting cold cream on the head and shaft of his
enormous prick, and also applying the same unguent to the
fundament† of his bride.

"What a pouting, rosy dimpled looking arse-quim you
have, Eveline dear, I shall have to use all my scientific knowledge to get in; but never fear, where there's a will, there's a
way. I will try very gently at first. Lucky your cunt is so far
behind. I can get at it best this way. Now, draw your breath,
darling, and push out your lovely arse to meet my thrusts.
Now ask me to fuck you properly this time."

"Don't you think, Eveline, dear, that the word 'fuck' is a
lovely expression," we heard him say. "Fuck—fuck—fucking,
is a heavenly way of speaking, and the word is so sacred to
love, that it is considered quite profane to mention it except
under such circumstances as the present. It is sacred to lovers
in the act of sexual enjoyment. Ask me to fuck you, love;
never mind your delicacy revolting against a word which is
usually considered improper for a lady to look at, even when
only chalked on a wall by some bad people, who delight in
outraging everyone's propriety. Shall I try to fuck you nicely
my love?"

"Yes, dearest; you know I love you so, but pray excuse the
natural timidity which I showed at the prospect of the first
attack of such a prick as yours. You see, dearest, I am trying
to please you by speaking in the language of love, for you

* "Woman's flesh sought for the satisfaction of male lust; loose women,
prostitutes collectively. Hence also: a woman's genitals; copulation. Now chiefly
in to hawk one's mutton: (of a woman) to flaunt her sexual attractiveness, to
solicit for lovers." (OED)
† *Unguent*: lubrication. *Fundament*: a humorous term for buttocks.

called your affair a prick, did you not? Now, dearest, although so tremulously afraid, I long to be fucked and made more and more a woman."

The enormous head of his prick when placed touching[46] Eveline's ravishing little tight hole, quite eclipsed our sight of its wrinkled beauties; and push hard as he might, it made no progress towards getting in, but always slipped off at a tangent.

He began to get furious, and ground his teeth with impatience, whilst Eveline, although trembling with lust and fear, gave vent to several painful groans, as he hurt her so much.

At length, again carefully adjusting the head of his tremendous battering ram to the spot, he clenched poor Eveline's hips with both hands pulling her arse towards him, pushing with great force at the same time, and we thought he really was getting into her.

"Ah! Ah—r—r—re! Oh, you'll murder me!" fairly screamed his bride. "Oh! I wish I'd never been married!" sobbing and crying as if her heart would break.

"Never mind dying first, only think of the pleasure to come dearest! But really if I kill you, or even myself, I am so excited and furious with lust, I must do it now," he exclaimed, his face crimson, and his eyes almost starting from his head.

But his efforts were quite unavailing.

"I'm damned if I can do it, although I've spent like a horse!" he said at last, withdrawing from the charge. "I only got in an inch, and it has nearly killed her."

We could see the spunk still bubbling from the head of his prick, which was slightly blood-stained, whilst his victim had really fainted, and lay showing the[47] effects of his attack, as we could distinctly see both blood and spendings smeared round and oozing from her arse-quim.

Lord Rasper looked non-plussed for a minute or so.

"By Jove! this will never do, to be beaten like a silly fool. I'll soon revive her, and try again," we could hear him say to himself.

He rang the bell impatiently, and then spoke through a tube to some one, and presently two cups of chocolate were brought to the door of the room; and received by his lordship without admitting the servant.

We noticed him put a few drops of brownish-looking fluid into each cup from a small bottle he took from his dressing case.[48] This, Lord Arthur whispered to me was "tincture of cantharides,"* adding, "we shall now see some real sodomite lust, when Eveline begins to feel[49] its effects, it will make her arse throb with such excitement she will suffer anything to be well fucked, and buggered till she faints or[50] even expires."

Having prepared the chocolate ready for his bride, he soon brought her round by applying a very powerful smelling bottle under her nose; how her lovely nostrils dilated as they sniffed up the fumes of the pungent salts, then, heaving a deep drawn sigh, her eyes opened.

"My love!" he exclaimed, "you're all right again, here's a beautiful cup of chocolate, it will do you a lot of good."

Presently she was thoroughly herself again, and took the cup from his hand.

"There, love!" he said, as he placed the empty cups on the table, "I won't try to fuck you again unless you ask me, as I know how painful it must have been to you. But we will try and have a nap in each other's arms for a few hours—perhaps to-morrow or some other day we may be able to consummate our happiness, my little darling countess."[51]

Eveline was all blushes, but taking her in his arms he stretched himself beside her lovely form upon the bed, and

* Also known as Spanish fly.

covered her with kisses, which she returned with almost equal ardour, but instead of going to sleep his hands tore aside the front of her dress, and took possession of the palpitating bosom of his bride.

"What lovely little bubbies, my darling, such charming little strawberry nosed nipples too; there was no occasion for you to wear a dress improver to make them look finer; these are just the size I love best. How they make my cock stand as I suck them. Does that excite you, Eveline, darling? What a sweet little hermaphrodite you are."

"Ah, oh, oh! Indeed you do, dearest. It is almost more than I can bear, your sucking my nipples sends such a thrill through my entire frame. I feel quite faint."

"Shall I play with your lovely little clitoris, my dear; see it's as stiff as my cock!" he said, slipping one hand down to her front, where we could see as he raised her dress that it stood up from the bush of golden auburn hair. How he gently frigged it, till the spendings spouted all over his hand [and] belly, and she wriggled her arse with excitement.

"You love, my own, my dearest sweetheart," she sighed, kissing him rapturously. "What shall I do? I want you so; do try and fuck me again. I will bear anything to make you happy. Kill me, if you like."

Lord Rasper's face beamed with pleasure. "Dearest," he said, "let us do or die this time; but I think if you kneel up on your hands and knees, and push out your bottom well, we shall manage to effect[52] our purpose."

She placed herself in position, and he once more anointed[53] the parts with cold cream, all the while he is doing so admiring the fine expanse of her lovely white round fat buttocks and saying, excitedly—

"That's right, get your knees well under your body, but rather wide apart. Ha! what a lovely moss rosebud quim you have, darling; how it throbs and contracts on my finger as I put the cold cream inside. It's as hot as a furnace, and moist with spendings. What a splendid white plump arse, the sight of it all is quite maddening! Oh, I must fuck you this moment, and make you a woman."[54]

"Go on, darling," said Eveline, "do fuck me now; I do want you so. Oh, if your finger was a little bigger what a darling little cock it would be; it puts me in such a flutter as you probe me with it. My bottom throbs with divine pleasure. Oh, do fuck me, for heaven's sake; don't play about with your finger any more. Oh! my bottom I believe is spending. Oh, my God".

His lordship's tremendous fiery-headed prick now presented his nose to the little wrinkled aperture, which we could actually see was twitching in lascivious expectation, so randy had the few drops of cantarides made his now actually lecherous bride.

The head of the monstrous prick slips in about an inch, but there he sticks by the shoulders again.

"Oh, give it me now, love. Oh, do push as I shove out my bottom! Push! ah! oh! push again! Oh! oh! Another inch! Oh! oh! Push, for God's sake; ram in, without mercy. Oh, heavens, oh!" she almost screamed, in her excitement.

Grasping her hips he gave a furious lunge, which got in two inches at least, but was so painful she really screamed in agony, writhing her bottom from side to side. But without heeding[55] her awful sufferings, he plunged on again and again shouting, "here goes the maidenhead at last!" till we could see drops of blood oozing from the orifice, as he withdrew just a trifle before each fucking plunge. Here her shrieks suddenly ceased for she had fainted, but only to revive in a minute or two to find him buried[56] to the hilt in the hitherto impregnable fortress of her virginity, which at[57] last was gone.

"My god, what agony! But it's slightly easier now. Hold me tight. Go on, my darling love; I feel your prick stretching my quim so deliciously, and the tickling of your bushy hair and bollocks against my crack drives me wild. Oh! oh! I am in a voluptuous delirium! I am a woman at last."

"Yes, and now I'm in, I guess I'll[58] stop there, as the big dog said to his little hot bitch," replied Lord Rasper, beginning to fuck with considerable energy, driving his hairy belly with force against her white arse, the smacking of flesh against flesh being very audible.

"How you spend, my darling, Ah (grunt); how you throb and nip my prick. Oh, oh! I'm coming now. Oh, Eveline, darling, can you feel[59] it pumping into you? Oh, how I love you. Oh, fuck! bugger! fuck! There, I shoot a baby into your womb".

"Oh, yes, my love; it is so delicious. It comes in great hot gushes, right up to my heart, and lifts my liver. Oh, oh, I swim in delight. I die, my love—hold me tight—fuck—fuck—fuck. Split me and kill me, you darling fucker. Let me dissolve in your hot spunk! Oh, oh!"

It was such an exciting finish that Lord Arthur carried me to the bed, tearing off my wreath, dress, and everything, and we had two long and madly voluptuous fucks.

Then, returning to our peep holes, we saw Lord Rasper, like a big dog fucking his bitch, still pegging away at his bride, who writhed and quivered in ecstasy under his fucking; her big arse wriggled sideways and every possible way, heaving backwards to meet his strokes, his prick, as it was pushed in and out, glistened with spendings, faintly tinted with rouge from the virgin blood which he had shed in his ruthless attack. They seemed to spend together two or three times, to judge by their wild lascivious motions, and exclamations of love and fondest endearment, with grunts of sensual rapture.

At length he withdrew, but only as it appeared to make an inspection of that lovely pouting arse-quim, which kept throbbing, opening and closing a little by spasmodic twitches every moment, the spunk oozing out, as we could plainly see, till carried away by his erotic passion, he kissed and tongued the wrinkled hole, making her scream out with excess of delight—

"Fuck me, fuck me again, my love. Oh, fuck and take me to heaven. I want you to split me and kill me, if you can! and be the victim of your lust, I love you so dearly."

"How you make me love and adore you more and more every moment, my own Eveline, my pet love," he exclaimed, as he at once proceeded to tear off her clothes, splitting the wedding dress, dragging the orange wreath and veil from her head, then his nervous hands rapidly demolished or tore away corset, skirts and all till, only drawers and chemise remained, and proceeded to unfasten the waistband of her drawers, pulling them off altogether, and rolling up her chemise. The whole expanse of his bride's lovely white plump buttocks was exposed to his gloating, lustful view. First amorously patting the splendid bottom, again he knelt down behind her and kissed every[60] part, tonguing[61] the divine little hole lasciviously, whilst one of his hands manipulated Eveline's magnificent clitoris so skilfully that she screamed with ecstasy and randy desire, pushing her arse-cunt against his mouth, challenging him by her lascivious motions, as we could hear her exclaim—

"Fuck me, Rasper my darling husband; your tongue sets my blood on fire, it tingles in every vein, from head to toe. Ah, now, do put him in again at once. Oh, oh! I'm spending once more; I melt in love and spunk my dearest darling husband!" as we could see the pearly jet boiling over his frigging fingers.

He was not slow to oblige her, and bringing the head of his prick[62] to the spot, again it glided in slowly, grunting as if he enjoyed the tightness, the lustful heat and the stretching[63] all the folds of that voluptuous sheath.

"How your darling cunt throbs, and nips me now. (grunt) Eveline, you like fucking now, don't you, my love (grunt)?"

"It's fine, it's so heavenly; push your precious jewel further and further in; rip, split, and bugger me to heaven. How I love to feel[64] it stretching and filling my quim with its grand proportions. If men only knew half the pleasures women experience, they would always want to be fucked. Oh, fuck— fuck—bugger—bugger—fuck. Oh, oh!"

They spent again in an agony of delight, and lay still for a minute or two, then Rasper falling over on his side, drew Eveline down with him.

"Now, darling," he said "let me show you an acrobat trick," as he lifted her left leg over his head and shoulder, and we saw him on the top of her in the most orthodox fashion, without for a moment losing his place in her quim. One arm tightly clasped her round the body, whilst his left hand kept posses- sion of Eveline's clitoris, which he frigged against his belly, as he went on with his fucking.

"Come to bed, darling," whispered Lord Arthur to me, "we shall never see the finish of them, no doubt they will go to sleep like that."

"You must fuck me again, dearest, before we go to sleep, and I will keep your dear prick in my cunt, ready for the first morning poke," I replied.

He adjusted two pillows under my arse and we had a most delicious long drawn out bout, he sucking my nipples till I was wild with lascivious lust, as I clung to him with arms and legs round his big back I seemed to fly or float with him in voluptuous delirium, as I called on him to keep on fucking me, and frig me too. It seemed a never ending one, but at last exhausted nature fixed us in delicious sleep in the very act of coition, leaving us to awake in the morning to finish the fuck.

Eveline shall tell you in a letter for herself the rest of our adventures, and also her awaking experiences next morning, which I was too much occupied to spy.

I have also left to her the relation of our reception by the members of Inslip's Club at the ball given in honour of our marriage, when we returned after the wedding trip. Besides, she had a delightful adventure with a spooney young fellow as we went across in the steamer from London to Antwerp.

How long I slept with Lord Arthur on the top of me, I don't know, but it was broad daylight when I first opened my eyes and realized the delightful situation. My clitoris clasped in his hand was still hard and stiff, and I could feel his grand prick right up me like a bar of hot meat, throbbing in my arse-cunt, which was gorged to repletion, glued to it by the profuse spendings of the previous night. The reminiscences of the past evening fired my blood in a moment, the sperm shooting from my cock-clitoris in a boiling jet.

It was too exquisite to awaken him abruptly, especially as he seemed in a most pleasant dream, his indistinct murmurs evidently having most endearing reference to voluptuous enjoyment; his prick throbbed till I could feel him spunking in reality right up to my vitals, whilst his hand pressed and frigged me delightfully, so throwing up my legs over his loins I heaved up my arse with the most complete abandon, making my quim contract with all[65] its power on his sensitive weapon, and commenced a splendid fuck, which he actually responded to in his sleep, and nothing but the final and almost volcanic ecstasy of spending again awoke my husband from what had seemed to him a delicious dream.

"Ah! Laura, my love, how exquisite, and to find it all real, too. My very soul melted into you just now," he ejaculated, as we rolled over, exhausted by the acme of our bliss.

His prick was so hardened that no amount of spending seemed to enervate it, and although my very entrails had been almost drowned by his tremendous rushes of hot boiling spunk, I longed and raved for more, like a perfect Messalina* of lust.

"Oh, my love," I gasped, "let me handle and suck your soul-stirring prick; let me drink down your luscious spendings, let me feel the delicious gush of it, as my tongue revels round the head of your prick!"

Then I suddenly disengaged myself from his embrace for the purpose of reversing our positions, when his prick was yet held so tightly by the sphincter muscle, and the clinging folds of my arse-cunt, that the "plop" of a champagne cork.

He buried[66] his face between my thighs, and "minetted" me splendidly with his tongue on my arse-cunt, which quivered and throbbed with emotion and excess of abandon. My whole nature seemed given out to him; my spendings flooded his hairy manly chest, and I furiously sucked the head of his big prick, rolling my tongue round and round, tickling the little orifice of the urethra, whilst my hands played with his hairy bollocks and the root of that splendid tool, till we were both so maddened with lust, that his sperm literally choked me by its copious and sudden discharge, whilst my very soul melted again on his manly bosom, as he sucked[67] and bit my quim with his teeth.

Once more he mounted me without delay, and we fucked ourselves to a voluptuous hysteria at last, as we screamed with delight, and lay in a confused heap on the bed, his prick buried[68] to the hilt, my arse-cunt holding him tighter than

---

* Probably a reference to Valeria Messalina (ca. 20-48 CE), the third wife of the Roman Emperor Claudius, who had a reputation for promiscuity.

ever, as the floods of spunk gushed far into the heart of my entrails.

No thing on earth can equal the delicious agonising ecstasy and voluptuous rapture of being fucked, caressed,[69] embraced, and treated as a real girl by a strong, hairy, lustful man, whose prick probes up to your heart, and makes us dissolve our very essence, as he strains you more and more in his brawny arms (whilst his big prick stirs every nerve and thrill of your body) to his warm, hairy, muscular form and Herculean body, palpitating with amorous lasciviousness. Oh, dear Louis, what unspeakable delights! No words can describe the intensity of such sensual raptures, for besides the exquisite pleasure of being fucked by a thundering big muscular prick, and drowned in its hot boiling love juice, there is the utter abandon of the passive enjoyment heightened by the unique piquancy of changing one's sex, and being changed into a woman.

Thus ended our first night of love, and I will leave Eveline to put the morning's finish to her night, merely adding that she told me poor Rasper was dreadfully skinned and sore, and too lame for love for a day or two.

May you have as much pleasure when your time comes to be married, is the best wish of your old friend.

LAURA.

LETTER

FROM

EVELINE TO LOUIS H——

DEAREST LOUIS,

Laura has made me keep her promise to you that I should copy from my journal the rest of our adventures on the wedding trip, and how we enjoyed ourselves at the grand ball given by the members of Inslip's Club in our honour when we returned.

You may be sure we slept well after the painful stretching and tearing of my wedding night, but I must say a little about the renewal of our delicious joys.

The next morning I was awakened lying in Rasper's embrace by a tremendous slap on my naked arse, by his spare arm, and opening my eyes in surprise, heard Rasper exclaim—

"Wake up, you lazy-cunted darling. Whatever you were before you lost your virginity, you are now my precious arse-fucking wife for life. Look at my thick hairy prick. Wake up, Eveline, love, and let's have a damned good fuck to give us an appetite for breakfast. What a lovely Sodomite bride you make, my love. My sweet darling Countess I must fuck you again."

Once thoroughly roused, all my blood was on fire for a renewal of our[70] overnight pleasures, and I kissed and tongued my husband passionately.

His enormous muscular ruby-headed prick stood before my eyes in all his glory, so grasping it[71] partly in my hand for it was too thick to take hold of all round, I gently caressed and frigged as it throbbed with excitement under my lascivious touches, till at last, carried away by a perfect abandon of lust, I took it in my mouth, and so gamahuched* him that my mouth was filled almost directly by a torrent of boiling sperm, which I swallowed with the greatest possible gusto. This only made him stiffer than ever; so making me kneel up on all fours again, he tried to put it into my tightly-wrinkled arse-cunt, which was now again as contracted as if that enormous prick[72] of his had never penetrated me.

"My God; be careful, Rasper, you'll really kill me this time. Oh, oh, oh! I can't stand it; you're bigger than ever, and I am so sore! Oh! oh!"

His efforts were fruitless, till again having recourse to the cold cream pot, and pushing with a kind of ferocious joy, he at last effected a very painful penetration. But, ye Gods, what joys repaid that pain. After he once spent his spunk into my arse-quim all went easy, and we revelled in lubricity, as I called on him to push his darling prick up to my heart; to stretch to split, to bugger, to fuck me to spend till I fainted from the very excess of emotion and became hysterical.

After this we had a double gamahuche till both spent in a perfect agony of delirium, and we rolled helpless and exhausted on the bed.

Nothing further of moment occurred[73] till we got on board the steamer for Antwerp,† and our husbands agreed that it would be a jolly idea for us brides to go in the ladies' cabin, whilst they had a cabin to themselves, and would keep an

---

* Another archaic sexual slang term for oral sex. In this case, fellatio.
† Customarily, the Victorian bride and bridegroom would leave for their honeymoon after the wedding breakfast.

eye on our adventures, and it was agreed that Laura should amuse herself with the girls, whilst I was open to flirt with any spooney young fellow whom I might attract.

When the Orion (that was the steamer's name)* cast off from the wharf, we were rather agreeably surprised to find the number of passengers very select; in fact, only a lady and gentleman, with two daughters of sixteen or seventeen, and a handsome young fellow, a son of about twenty; and, what was more to our purpose, evidently, one who had an eye to the ladies, one of those really handsome fellows that many young married ladies or single girls at once fell in love with.

We soon became chatty with the two daughters, whilst our husbands amused papa and mamma. After passing Gravesend we all four retired to the ladies' cabin to prepare for dinner.

"And you two are brides, only married yesterday?" enquired one of them called Bertha. "And did you find it so very delightful last night?"

"Yes; would you like to know all about it? Don't you long to be married, too?"[74]

"Yes, I think so, sometimes; and yet I am afraid."

"Afraid of what, dear?" I enquired.

"Why, a big man might hurt me so," she replied.

"Oh, fie; nonsense; it's[75] nothing so dreadful. But what a handsome young fellow your brother is."

"Yes" said Stella, the other sister. "Pray be careful of him; he's a dreadful boy after all the girls, and married ladies too. I saw him looking particularly at you"[76]

"Did you, my dear?" I replied. "Now would you like to teach him a lesson?[77] it would be such fun if you would help me. Let me think. Suppose you tell him I admire him very

---

* There was a steamship called the Orion which went down on 17 June 1850 on a sailing from Liverpool to Glasgow. Any connection between that ship and *Letters* is not immediately apparent.

much, so as to egg him on just a little; and if he takes the bait, it will be such fun."

"Oh, I am[78] for it," she answered. "Herbert thinks so much of himself, he wants taking down just a trifle. But don't make your husband jealous, or create a row."[79]

"I'll let him into the secret, so that there shall be no harm."

Lord Arthur and my husband kept on the bridge with the captain smoking and drinking champagne. Laura and the sisters promenaded the deck together, and as it was getting dusk, I slipped into the smoking saloon—a little cabin luxuriously fitted up on deck for gentlemen's use. It was quite empty, so I disposed myself for a snooze on the soft cushions of the seats, but had scarcely done so before Herbert, smoking[80] a cigar, sauntered in.

"Oh, pardon me, lady," he exclaimed, pretending to be taken by surprise. "Don't let me disturb you; I can smoke outside."

"No, no; it's me, who has no business here. Pray don't let me drive you outside. But, really, my husband seems to like the captain's society so much more than mine.[81] I came here to think over his indifference, after being married only one day," I said with a deep sigh.

"How inconsiderate; what can you expect from such a beginning. How I wish I was your husband; you'd find me follow you like a lap dog," was his remark.

"But when lap dogs come to be your master they turn to bull dogs, I'm afraid,"[82] I said, with a faint sigh.

You should have seen him throw away his cigar and fall at my feet, whilst I was apparently too much taken by surprise to resist his taking possession of my hand, and covering it with warm amorous kisses.

"Fie! for shame, Sir!" I presently exclaimed, trying to draw my hand from his grasp. "My husband might come!"

"No fear of that," he said, with a rather subdued laugh. "He's too pleased with the captain's company, and is nearly tight.* Even if he returns to his cabin it will be only as a sottish imbecile. Beautiful lady, did you but know how your transcendent[83] beauty has captivated my heart you would have some pity for my feelings; besides, you know:[84] 'What the eye doesn't see, the heart won't grieve,'† is a very true saying."[85]

By this time his roving hands had possessed themselves of one foot, and was even caressing[86] the calf, as he rapturously kissed my boots and ancles.

"Well," I sighed, with an assumed shiver of emotion, "If I do flirt with you a little while, it is only to have my pique out for his indifference. But, Sir, pray sit properly by my side, and don't take such foolish liberties".[87]

"How can I help it, you darling love?" he exclaimed, getting up, and putting his arm round my waist, as he sat down by my side, not forgetting now it was almost dark, to imprint several very warm kisses on my lips and cheeks.

"Pray don't; you make me so confused," I said, with suppressed emotion, and making a faint effort to disengage myself from his embrace one of my hands designedly touched just where I knew his talisman of love was to be found. What a fine one it seemed, and hard and excited too, as I felt it very distinctly throb under my gentle pressure. How to seduce the seducer? that was now[88] the question with me.

"Oh, heavens! what shall I do? You hold me so tight, and kiss me so rudely. Pray let me go, Sir, or I really must do something desperate, or scream out."

His only answer was a desperate attempt to get his hands

* Drunk.
† This saying dates to the 14th century, but it is found almost verbatim in J. L. Burckhardt's *Arabic Proverbs*, published in 1830.

under my clothes, and he really got one as far as my thigh.

"You love; you drive me mad with desire! I would die rather than not have you now. Why make such resistance and scandal, when nobody can know if you are only discreet. Dearest lady, let me perform your husband's duty whilst he is neglecting you?"

"I can't; pray don't press me. I really cannot do it. You promise never to divulge my secret, but the fact is my husband says I'm an hermaphrodite, as much man as woman, although the plumpness[89] of my bosom indicates I am a female. I believe in his heart he's disgusted with me already," I said, in faltering accents and then burst into a sobbing fit, as if thoroughly distressed.

"Darling creature, whatever you are, you make me more madly in love with you than ever. Let me soothe your grief."

His insinuating hand now found my clitoris, which was as hard as his own priapus, and I could feel his fingers playing with it in such a way as to make me long to have him.

"Isn't it awful to have such a malformation?"[90] I sighed. "Every man will be disgusted with me!"

"No, no, never, for my part; the touch of your clitoris gives me exquisite pleasure, and fills me with such curious longings. Do, darling lady, take the same liberty with me," he replied, placing one of my hands on his prick, which he had let out of his trousers.

I felt it so beautifully stiff, and feeling like warm ivory. But in a moment my touch brought him to a crisis, and my fingers were bedewed by his profuse emission, as he gave a deep sigh of pleasure.

"Now, let me fuck you, dear lady," he whispered; "you really cannot love that indifferent husband of yours, and I will give you such pleasure."

"Well, now I have allowed you such freedom, Mr.

Herbert—you see I know your name—I will tell you exactly what I have fallen out with Lord Rasper about. You see he fucked me the first, and put me to such exquisite pain with his great rolling pin of an affair—quite a donkey's, I assure you—that I insisted he should let me put my clitoris in his arse-hole and serve him the same. That's where we split, and no man shall ever fuck me again who refuses me the same favours that he requires from me."

"And may I fuck you, if I let you have my bottom first?" he enquired.

"Certainly, and upon no other terms," I replied, squeezing his cock in my fingers so amorously that he almost jumped with the sudden pain.

"Now, to business; down with your trousers, if you accept my terms, and you will find I can frig your cock deliciously at the same time; and[91] it must give you the same pleasure I feel when my big clitoris is caressed."

"Your soft hand is delightful, and I have quite a fancy to feel like a woman for once: I have so often wondered what it can be like to feel a cock in one's inside, stirring up and stretching your arse till you feel mad with delight; for I know the women really experience much more pleasure than a man. A young girl will spend three or four times to my once, and I'm anything but slow."

By the time his trousers were down, and kneeling in front of him I kissed and caressed his lovely prick, taking its soft head between my lips and sucking it, at the same time rolling my tongue round it in the most lascivious manner, my hands playing with his balls, and postillioning[92] his bottom hole till he again spent in my mouth such an aromatic flavoured flood of spunk, which made me come, too.

"Now, dear, lean over the seat, and push out your bottom, and clitty shall do her best to take your virginity."[93] Then, standing behind him, with my skirts turned up to my waist, I took hold of his hips, and drew his splendid arse close to my belly, and pointing my cocky straight to his tightly wrinkled bum hole, all slippery as it was with spendings, I soon got the head in, and although he fairly groaned with the pain, soon drove myself right in up to the roots of my hair. Being securely in possession, I rested a minute or so to feel and examine the beauties of his posteriors, which seemed to my hands (as I felt in the dark) to have quite a feminine development, so soft, fleshy, and yet firm as marble, his sphincter muscle all the while nipping my delighted cock in quite a series of lascivious throbs, and his whole body seemed to quiver with delight, as he gasped in a suppressed voice his impatience for me to begin. My hands roved in front, feeling his fine, stiff prick, and passed down to his hairy[94] manly balls, which I gently pressed between my fingers.

"You drive me mad, dearest. Oh, go on, and fuck me well," he ejaculated. "The feelings I experience at being thus, as it were, changed to a woman beggar description—so voluptuous, so lascivious. Feel how I am spending. Fuck me. Rub the spunk up and down my prick with your soft hand. Ah, ah, your prick, I mean your clitoris, swells deliciously; how delightful, it is to have my arse hole stretched like that to its utmost limit. Your hair tickles it so excitingly every time you push in, and your belly smacks so voluptuously at every push on my rump. Push further, stretch me, split me, you love. Ye Gods, now I feel spouting into my very entrails the balm of love. Fucking a woman is nothing so exquisite as the continued long drawn out bliss I feel now; may I always be a woman and feel such ecstasy."

Holding him tight we galloped on to another finish, my lunges making him fairly gasp and cry out in his wild ecstasy; and when I came again, instead of assuaging our lust, we fairly quivered from the excess of our libidinous desires, which seemed insatiable. His tight bottom was a throbbing furnace, juicy, with mucous spendings, the maddening pressures and contractions of its inner folds driving me to such an excess of lubricity, that I started on another course, and never finished till with[95] mingled cries of erotic agony we sank exhausted on the seat and rolled to the floor, when we were suddenly brought to our senses by some one lighting a fusee, and Laura's silvery laugh at once disclosed who it was that had surprised us.

"I thought I would warn you to be more careful; your acclamations of delight attracted me. I'm Eveline's friend, Mr. Herbert, so the little secret is quite safe. Ta ta, my dear; you'll come into the ladies' cabin soon, I suppose, or there may be a scandal!" saying which Laura was gone.

Herbert was covered with confusion, but was soon reassured, especially when I told him that Laura was an hermaphrodite like myself, and that I would introduce him to her when we got to Brussels. We sat spooning in the dark for some time, but he was too pumped out to have the fuck I had promised him, so with the first glimmer of dawn in the east we slipped away to our cabins.

It was my turn now to surprise Laura, with Bertha and Stella—she was actually fucking one and kissing the cunt of another on the floor of the cabin.[96] How the two girls sprang up with fright, but they were soon made to understand it was all right with me, so I slipped into a berth to sleep whilst they finished their fun.

Nothing of moment worth writing about occurred[97] till we took up our apartments in a large hotel in the Rue Royale,[98] near the old English Bank.*

---

* The Old English Bank and Exchange Office was at 8 Rue Royale and assisted English travellers with monetary needs while abroad.

Rasper and Lord Arthur were both quite fresh after the sea air and one night's rest, and proposed to show each other the beauties of their brides. Our rooms opened one into the other, so after retiring for the night Lord A. called us into his room, and they both acted as our lady's maids.

"Now," said his lordship, "what do you think of Lady Laura?" when he had stripped her of every thing but chemise and drawers, &c.

"What lovely brown hair; and look at her firm little bubbies. Oh, such delicious ones to suck, and see, too, now I take off her chemise and drawers, what a lovely clitoris she has, it's[99] a perfect little devil of randiness, always wet with spendings. You can't touch my darling without making her come."

My husband also removed my chemise and every thing that could obstruct a view of my charms. Then they compared our hair, by letting down and combing out the long plaits till it covered our bottoms; this seemed to give them exquisite pleasure.

My bubbies were quite as large as Laura's, and my blue eyes and auburn hair made a delightful contrast to hers.

Next we had to lean over the edge of the bed, and Lord Arthur expatiated on our various charms.

"Look, Rasper," he said, "what a lovely arse-cunt Lady Laura has, it is such a lovely brown tint, with soft wrinkles, and the least little caresses cause it to throb with emotion. Look at the lovely slight fringe of brown hair all round it, getting thicker lower down till it covers the balls of her clitoris, and makes quite a curly, silky bush on her mount in front. Look at her stiff clitoris see the ruby head is even now bubbling over with spendings. Taste how deliciously pungent the flavour is, and I will do the same to Lady Eveline."

He opens the cheeks of my bottom, and minettes with his tongue my pinky wrinkled rose-bud cunt as he calls it, which so excited me that my spunk fairly spurted over the bed, and on his fingers as he caressed my clitoris.

Presently he went on again—

"Did you ever see two such lovely voluptuously white feminine arses, so deliciously fat, round, and plump? What a swell of hip and thigh, how it makes your prick stand at the very thoughts of the delights to be sucked or fucked out of their rosebud cunts; the very sight of so many charms drives me wild with lust, makes me in a flutter all over. Let us fuck each other's wives for a change?"

"With all my heart!" replied my husband. "I'm longing to fuck your Laura, and the tighter her quim the more pleasure for my prick."

Saying which he placed Laura in an easy chair, and began by gamahuching her clitoris so amorously I thought he would suck it off. Then, after a little, putting cold cream on their parts, he placed himself in the chair, and asked her to fix herself on his prick.

Lord Arthur took me on his lap, and sat playing my clitoris, whilst I gently frigged his fine, manly cock, as he asked me to wait and see how his friend Rasper would manage to get his enormous battering-ram into Laura's tight hole, and then we can have our fuck.

"Eveline, darling, I long to taste the sweets of your golden-haired fanny."

Meanwhile Laura did not find it so easy to take in Rasper's prick, we could see by the pained expression on her face that he was hurting her awfully, in fact, he stuck just as he had with me the first time.

Poor Laura bit her lips till the blood came to suppress her cries, but all in vain, for his lordship at once clasped her with all his muscular strength, and pressing her down by the hips, partly got into her quim, making her scream with pain.

This so excited him that he ruthlessly shoved up, and pulled or pressed her down at the same time, and we saw him gradually gain ground, till his big prick was sheathed to its roots, as he ground his teeth and held her like in a vice.

"Put her on the bed, and I'll adjust a pillow under her arse!" exclaimed Lord A. "Let her have it properly, now you are in, Rasper."

This was soon done, and my partner whispering in my ear, I attacked the arse-hole of my husband, which was a lovely dark-brown wrinkled hole. My cock-clitoris was in fine order, and slippery with spendings, so in spite of his calling out that I was hurting him, I pushed on up to the hilt, and putting my arms round his waist, felt his prick as he began to fuck Laura; at the same time Lord Arthur succeeded in getting into me, and the four were linked together in one glorious fuck, each one in the other, except Laura's clitoris, which I frigged with one hand, whilst my other caressed my husband's prick as he worked it in and out of her tight quim. It was both man and woman at once, such exquisite sensations pervaded my whole frame; my arse gorged and stretched most voluptuously by Lord Arthur's fine prick, whilst I repaid him by all the lascivious nippings and contractions of the sheath to increase his lubricity; whilst as to myself a perfect fury of desire impelled me to do the same to my husband, the voluptuous sensations of possession as his glowing arsehole contracted and throbbed on my swelling cock, was so inexpressibly delicious that I spent at least three times in rapid succession, and the others being equally excited, our final spend was accompanied by a perfect volley of lascivious expressions—such as.

"Fuck, fuck. Oh, bugger! bug-ger! Kiss me, darling. I'm coming. Oh! oh! How gloriously you spend in my arse. Fuck me! Bugger me! Oh, sodomy! Oh! oh! oh!"

After this we all tumbled in a confused heap on the bed,

sucking gamahuching and frigging till there was a not a drop of spend left in any of us, and we lay throbbing and still palpitating with our raging unsatisfied desires.

I shall now merely say that Herbert was introduced to Laura and our husbands, who admitted him to one or two of our midnight orgies, and found him an agreeable and piquant change, so much so, that being desirous of introducing him as a new member at Inslip's, he made some excuses to his parents, and returned with us to London.

Laura and I went several times to hear the band in the park, and our English beauty seemed very much to impress Messrs. les Bruxellois, who paid us most marked attentions, rubbing their knees against us, pressing our toes with their feet, and even feeling our bottoms and thighs through our dresses whenever they had a chance of sitting close enough to us, but we contented ourselves with having seduced Herbert.

On our return to town Inslip's ball was to come off at once, every member had promised to be present, as well as the sixteen bridesmaids who had assisted at our wedding.

You may guess we looked forward to it with considerable anticipation of pleasure, as we had been given to understand that our sixteen bridesmaids were all to be there, and in the orgie after dancing would be ravished nolens-volens* by their male partners.

Before giving an account of the ball I must speak of the address which Archdeacon Vaseline opened the proceedings with.

As soon as we had entered the ball room he took for his text "Les delices de Sodome sont chers à lui comme agent comme passif."†

* Whether willing or not (*OED*).
† "Sodom's delights are as dear to him in their active as in their passive form."
From de Sade's first dialogue in *Philosophy in the Bedroom*.

"My beloved ones of both and all the sexes, I do not even intend to allude to such a common place subject as fucking a cunt—cunt being altogether at a discount in this distinguished assembly, but it is my privilege and duty as your priest and spiritual adviser on this occasion to give you a short address, founded on the second page of our great master the Marquis de Sade, called 'La Philosophie du Boudoir,' in which, speaking of that enthusiastic votary of Sodom, Monsieur Dolmancé, he says that to him, 'the delights of Sodom were equally dear both as agent and patient,' and after a few remarks on this most interesting subject I shall finish with an exhortation to those two darling brides to do their duty in the new state of life to which they have been called, and then to the bridesmaids to follow their charming example on the earliest possible occasion, and conclude with my priestly benediction on these newly-married couples.

"First, then, my darling ladies, Laura and Eveline, you must now realise that you have become the brides of two devotedly attached husbands, and you will be expected to submit yourselves wholly to their desires, wishes, or whims, and to have for the future no other object but to give your persons up to their love and lust—the only exception being when you come to the club meetings with them, and, for these times at least, you have full leave and absolution to enjoy the society of others, and give up your charms to the enjoyment of the members who meet you here on such solemn occasions.

"Now, after these preliminary remarks, I will return to the subject of my text.

"First note that to the experienced votary of Sodom, the active and passive joys are equally dear. I know there are many here who have tried both, and that some will perhaps prefer the active joys of Sodomy. It is, indeed, a great and ineffable pleasure to have a glorious big prick, ten or twelve inches long, like this (here he brings his own out, and flashes its grand proportions in the face of the excited company, an acolyte kneeling down in front of him, and gently frigging it, so as to sustain the erection to the end of his address) throbbing with lustful expectations, the spunk boiling in the tightly pursed up balls beneath, at the view of a round plump white arse before, it, whether masculine or feminine, although the former is[100] vastly to be preferred; and to know that such a superb mass of white human flesh is ready "for the knife," only too eagerly waiting for the fierce red-headed monster of a prick to be plunged up to the hilt; then my darlings, to open wide those delicious buttocks, to see the divine, rosy, little hole, to kiss and prepare it for the dreaded ordeal, and then to present the flaming head one's impatient prick to its wrinkled, twitching tight orifice! Ah! it is as much as a man can do to prevent spending in anticipation! But, to go on, with[101] great efforts at last the head gets in, then by strenuous efforts, and hard ramming, drawing the darling's haunches firmly towards one, the huge prick gradually forces his way in, in spite of the wriggles, writhings, and screams of the victim, until at last every fold and ridge of the sensitive membrane lining this tight, hot, delicious altar of love has been opened and stretched, and the proud, swelling conqueror lies embedded in the very heart of the darling's entrails, returning throb for throb.

"Ah, then who can describe the exquisite sensations of triumph that possesses that happy prick, as he throbs and feels himself the victor of another arse-maidenhead—another virginity has fallen to his prowess, the prostrate[102] quivering arse, and shuddering frame of the vanquished victim attesting his success.

"But I am afraid I may frighten the bridesmaids, who have favoured us this evening with their company to do honour to the return of our sweet brides at this club ball, where they must be prepared for anything that may happen. I say, considering this, I will now pass on to discuss the second part of my text—'the passive enjoyments of the delights of Sodom.'

"Ah, my friends, who that is only a little voluptuous, does not feel his heart throb and body thrill with lust, when he thinks of what this[103] means—as De Sade says, how[104] delicious and exquisite beyond the power of words to express, is the act of giving up and changing one's sex and becoming a woman, to be the mistress of a man, who treats you exactly as a girl, to counterfeit and imitate all the impulses, feelings, and desires of an amorous woman to her lover, to give one's self up to him and other lovers, body and soul, to be caressed, cherished, embraced, felt, cuddled, and fondled as a pretty woman by a longing lover, or husband, then after the sweet preliminary toyings and caresses are over, to give oneself[105] up to him, then to present the chief object of his worship, to be felt and kissed, to feel his dear tongue tickling the tight little throbbing pouting hole, then after a maddening titillation[106] increased by his whiskers and moustache rubbings against the tender, sensitive, little orifice, to feel him get upon his knees, and bring the lustful monster of a prick to the charge. Oh, my friends, who can properly describe the delicious agony, the heavenly pain of those entrancing moments, when, embraced tightly in his brawny arms, the huge hot brute is forcing his way in! to feel him breaking through every obstacle, pushing his hard, hot mass of throbbing prick further and further in, till the hot friction and stretching of every ridge and fold of the sensitive membrane causes the first shudder of approaching bliss to be felt, when at last the swelling conqueror, landed to his full length (perhaps a foot) with his huge head, swelling and throbbing more and more, hot gushes of boiling spunk inundate your very vitals, or, as we might better call it your gasping womb, and you feel at least several pounds of hot meat choking and gorging your rectum vagina. I say as you lie quivering with lust, strained tight in his Herculean arms to his hairy, warm body. What thrills and emotions stir your inmost soul, as he spunks his very essence into your entrails.

"No woman ever feels the joys of coition like passive Sodomite, for the exquisite sensitiveness of the lining membrane and folds of the arse-vagina far exceed in intensity those thrilling delights which a good prick is supposed to excite in a truly voluptuous woman. The Hermaphrodites of ancient times were really the types of this delicious double sexuality which the passive Sodomite enjoys, for whilst the arse-quim is so rapturously fucked by a huge hot rampant prick, the fucker's hands can frig the cock-clitoris so as to double the ecstasy of spending, and even enhance the very acme of bliss, only to be obtained when the sexes come together.

"Beautiful brides and lovely bridesmaids, let me exhort you all, the first to continue, and the second to make haste to begin these luscious experiences, such as even the angels in heaven long to enjoy.

"Then, again, think of the double pleasure you can experience in both fucking and being fucked at the same time; for where many are gathered together as my dear friends are here to-night, each one can link on to the arse of his partner in front, whilst another obliges him in the same way behind; your own prick revelling in the contracting folds of a delighted arse-quim before you, revelling, I may say, in all the delights of possession, whilst you feel[107] a thundering, randy, hot-headed cock, stretching and filling every fold of your own arse, spending torrents of boiling sperm right up to your heart, and almost poking its head out at your naval.

"My tongue fails further to describe the delights of feeling of both male and female in one, lavishing every caress and endearment on the girl you are fucking, and yet being treated, fondled, and fucked as a girl yourself.

"I can only finish by saying let us make haste to experience all this!"

At the conclusion of the Archdeacon's address, which was received with rapturous applause and lascivious excitement,[108] Mr. Inslip and Count R—— formally introduced us to the ball room, where the latter claimed me whilst the Archdeacon did the same by Lady Laura for the first quadrille.*

General Wilkes danced with Miss Honeydew, a lovely blonde of seventeen, dressed in dead white satin petticoat, trimmed lace flounces, train, panier,† and bodice of light mauve velvet, elegantly trimmed with lace, her arms encircled in rows of costly pearls, and the same innocent-looking but precious jewels entwined her swelling throat, whilst an aigrette of diamonds and pearls set off the glory of her sunny auburn hair. She was the General's partner; Captain Bull standing up with another bridesmaid, Miss Curley, a little piquante brunette of sixteen, elegantly dressed in clouds of primrose gauze, dead gold ornaments on her arms, neck, and ears, a bunch of dark red roses in her bosom, and one or two set off her raven hair. She had the tiniest of sleeves imaginable, leaving her pretty shoulders, arms, and bosom very much exposed.

These made up our set, but before saying more about that let me give a short description of the other bridesmaids, who with Selina and Isabel,‡ fairly filled the ball-room with a

---

* A square dance performed typically by four couples and containing five figures, each of which is a complete dance in itself.

† A frame used to expand a woman's dress at the hips. A common fashion in the Victorian period.

‡ Selina and Isabel first appear in *Sins*. They are Frederick Park and Fred Jones, respectively. See *Sins*, p. 50 and p. 36, respectively.

galaxy of feminine beauty, making in all a splendid company of forty ladies and gentlemen. The latter, I ought in justice to observe were most of them fine or very handsome fellows as any one could wish for in affairs of love.

The sixteen lovely girls who had acted as our brides-maids, and now graced by their presence the club ball given to welcome us back to town, consisted of eight dark and eight very fair young ladies, who had been selected by the members of the club for the especially feminine contour of their persons, every one of them possessing in perfection lovely bosoms and splendid arses as far as one could judge of them in full dress, but more anon, and as they floated round the ball room in the arms of their male partners to the strains of the mazy waltz, they looked lovely specimens of feminine beauty.

Miss Brompton was a seductively fair wench; Miss Honey-dew I have described; then there were Miss Vincent, Miss Grove, and Miss Offer, all blondes of the fairest type, with deep-blue eyes, coral lips, and pearly teeth, displayed when-ever they smiled; Mdlle. Natica was a rather reddish-auburn haired Russian beauty, imported by Count K—— from Livonia, her hazel eyes speaking volumes of voluptuous ideas, if one but took the trouble to study her face, which was otherwise rather pale, but beautifully outlined. Miss Connie and Miss Sparkler were light-brown haired beauties, with those big grey eyes which denote greediness in affairs of cock and cunt. As to the brunette eight, in addition to Miss Curley, there came little Miss Pover, very petite, with piercing dark eyes; then a Circassian beauty from Constan-tinople, called Fatima, a splendid, lovely, imperious looking creature, with cheeks like damask roses, and raven hair; Signora Diva, a superbly developed Italian beauty; Mdlle. Drusilla, a French Jewess, who looked as if she would let a man fuck her and cut his head off afterwards, if necessary to act like Judith;* Miss Mostyn was a proud, aristocratic looking girl, tall, and graceful as a swan,[109] her low dress displaying quite a ravishing display of bubbies; Miss Dancy, a dark-eye flirt, always looking after the gentlemen; and, last of all, Miss Gordon, a sweet good-natured[110] girl, just one of the sort who can refuse nothing from a promise to marry, to a good stiff prick, as she never likes to hurt any one's feelings.

They were all dressed the same, one costume for the blondes, and another for the brunettes.

"Now, Lady Eveline," whispered the Count after the quadrille, he is such a handsome fellow, one loses your heart to him in a moment; "did you find Lord Rasper all you could wish, dear?"

"Decidedly; rather more than I could have wished for!" I replied, with a smile, laying one of my hands (which held my fan) down on his thigh, so as to touch and find that his manly mechanism was wound up to the highest pitch of erotic[111] tension, the main cylinder throbbing with emotion under the weight of my hand.

"Would mine have suited you better do you think? Oh, Lady Eveline, I do love you so; won't you pet the head of the slave who is anxious to be let loose, and be caressed?"

As he spoke he somehow managed to slip the naked truth into my hand, all gloved as it was snatching away my fan at the same moment. I turned away my eyes, afraid to look, but all the same convulsively pressed his prick for him, with a gently frigging motion; one of his hands was under my

* The Book of Judith is a deuterocanonical text of the Old Testament in which Judith decapitates the Assyrian general Holofernes. She charms her way into his tent and he foolishly falls asleep, giving Judith the opportunity to cut his head off, thus allowing Israel to counter-attack Assyria.

clothes, groping and trying to force its way between my tightly pressed thighs.

"Oh, for shame, Count; how can you be so rude as to try and seduce me so soon after marriage?[112] Suppose my husband should see it. Pray, put it out of sight. Oh, indeed, you shan't get your hand up there!" as I made quite a strong[113] resistance to his bold advances.

Just then his prick seemed almost to bound in my hand, and the spendings shot all over my arm in warm drops of luscious juice, which so affected me that my thighs relaxed, and his hand seized my fanny, clitoris, and all, only to find his fingers wetted with the emission I could not restrain under such exciting circumstances.

"Forgive me, darling; how could I help myself after such an exciting quadrille. But now," he said, rising, "let me get you some refreshment, then au revoir till the fun after the dancing, for I fancy the beautiful bridesmaids will find themselves slightly altered before we allow them to go home from the ball."

Here the band struck up a waltz, and I got another partner.

Several more quadrilles, waltzes, polkas, &c., were gone through, each one followed by a rest in one of the alcoves, so convenient for spooning. At length they gave over the terpsichorean exercise, and the band of musicians retired, and supper was announced. After a splendid and brilliant repast, with any amount of the very best champagne, a large, wide backless couch, big enough to accommodate any number of people, was wheeled into the centre of the ball room, right under the chandelier. Here every gentleman brought his partner, and the light being lowered[114] till the apartment was almost in darkness, a general osculation[115] commenced all round, and Mr. Inslip gave us a small ball, to be passed from one to the other, whilst Lord Arthur was set the task of finding it, the person so caught with it in his or her possession to be at once stripped for the inspection of the company.

His lordship glided round and round as active as a cat, pretending to pounce upon it every now and then. First he caught the Archdeacon, declaring he could feel it in his trousers, and only appeared satisfied when he had groped his reverend prick to a spend. Then Miss Brompton, one of the prettiest of the bridesmaids, very fair, with quite a Grecian face, would not allow him to look for it under her clothes.

"No, no; you shan't; you nasty man. How dare you, Sir?' she exclaimed, indignantly, trying to push him away; but we all came to his assistance, and her lovely blue dress was torn to ribbons in a moment. Then corset, everything she had on in fact torn off, as we declared she had the ball between her legs. Nothing presently remained but her drawers to protect her virginity from our indecent assaults. Up went the light— and there she was fighting and struggling the Count trying to force his hand into the slit in her drawers, as she desperately crossed her legs.

"Oh! A—r—r—re! You wretches! I'll bite you!" she screamed, trying to fix her teeth in my hands, as I helped to hold her down.

"Bravo, Count!" said Lord Arthur, "find the ball and you shall have the obstinate girl's maidenhead."

Her legs were opened by force, and, oh! such a lovely cock clitoris rewarded our efforts. Then the drawers were torn to shreds, and we could see such a splendid expanse of hip, promising a superb display of buttocks, when we turned her over.

Lord A. pointed out all her naked charms one by one. First the swelling bubbies, set off by little rosy nipples; then the small waist and voluptuous hips; the lily-white skin of her belly set off by a delicately mossy mount of light-auburn hair, from which sprang the stiff, ruby-tipped clitoris which Count K—— was playing with, kissing its head taking it between his lips, till we presently saw by the quivering emotions of the young lady that she had come to a crisis, the flood of sperm shooting into his delighted mouth, and even oozing over his moustache in pearly drops, as he sucked the head of her affair.

"Now, turn her over," said Lord A., and at once we had a view of[116] all her posterior charms, for she was regularly spread-eagled by us holding her legs and arms so that she was helpless. The Count was in ecstasies, her white fat bottom projecting over the edge of the couch enabled him to kneel down and press his lips to the rosy wrinkled arse-quim; as he opened the crack with his hands; then we saw his tongue busy lubricating the delicious aperture which promised his prick such a harvest of delights. This made her squirm and wriggle with emotion, and she almost screamed when he put his finger in with some cold cream.

"Ah—ah—no! How disgusting! Will none of you save me from being outraged so?" she screamed, in agony.

"Make a woman of her, Count," said some, "your prick is in fine order!"[117]

He got up, his flaming courser standing out in front, where his open trousers showed a glorious growth of curling brown hair round its roots and well pursed-up manly balls.

Lady Laura held the cold cream pot, and putting a little on the head of his fine pego, it was presented to the rosy wrinkled aperture of Miss Brompton's arse-cunt. Some one was frigging her clitoris, so clasping her hips with both hands, he drew her arse to meet his attack, and so pushed that he gained quite two inches at once. Then again, and again, he rammed his prick in, till his splendid balls spanked against the entrance, exclaiming—

"Here goes her maidenhead, and I am into her up to her navel, which, my God, I am rubbing against."

She was mad with rage and shame; but, heedless of her cries, he only rested about a minute, to enjoy the delightful sense of a thorough possession, making his prick throb in the tight sheath, till we could see Miss Brompton's eyes show a strange kind of light in them, as he began to raise all the lustfulness of her warm nature. How she blushed and ground her teeth, closing her eyes as she noticed we knew she was enjoying it.

The Count fucked her deliciously, and spending almost directly, cried out to her—

"My darling! you love! What pleasure you gave me; do you feel me[118] spending into you now? That's it, wriggle your splendid arse; what lovely sidetwists you put on, dear Miss Brompton. How your cunt now sucks at my enraptured prick in at every push! Ah! ah! Ah—r—r—re! I'm coming again, you darling!"

Miss B. could restrain herself no longer, twisting and squirming about in extatic voluptuousness, we could see his beautiful prick withdrawn and sucked in at every return stroke,[119] whilst their mixed mucous spendings and sperm dripped in thick creamy drops as[120] the piston of love worked in and out.

"How lovely! dear Count; fuck me well now; you do indeed touch my navel; I can feel the hot burning head there at every thrust! I forgive every thing, only do fuck me, frig me, make me come; spend into me your darling juice! Oh, heavens! I shall die of delight; my sensations are more than I can bear. Your lovely prick fills and stretches me so. Go on—go on. Oh! pray, don't stop!" &c., she almost screamed, in her agony of delight; at last she swooned right off.

Meanwhile our husbands conducted Laura and myself to

two couches in the centre of the room, and if I give my own experience you will know that Laura had the same treatment and enjoyed herself quite as much; in a minute or two Lord Rasper and myself were both perfectly naked, and he laid me with my belly on the couch, and with my bottom just projecting over the lower end two pillows were placed under my breast and belly to raise my head a little; then, taking my legs under his arms, I felt the head of his big prick poking at my rosy arse-cunt behind; five other gentlemen now came up to join our friendly party, and five others assisted Lord Arthur with Lady Laura. Herbert presented his lovely prick to my lips, Captain Bull and General Wilkes placed their rampant and swelling ruby-headed cocks in my hands to frig, and two others fucked me under the armpits. It was a wonderful undertaking to have to manage six pricks at once, but my soul was in it, and Lord Rasper filling and stretching my arse-quim to its utmost capacity, aroused every atom of voluptuousness within me. I squirmed and wreathed my arse from side to side, his delicious thrusts filling me with more and more of erotic fury at every shove.

My lips took in Herbert's prick and my tongue rolled around the head of the delicious morsel; my nimble fingers fairly skinned the pegos[121] they held, I rubbed them up so rapidly, and yet with a soft touch, such as none but an accomplished woman can apply or understand the mystery of.

The pricks worked under my arms gave me an indescribable feeling, their rubbing their noses in the soft silky hair, then poking against my bubbies, made me so ravenous for fucking that I seemed to want every one in my quim at once, I felt pricks all over me—gorged with pricks, in fact—every pore of my body wanted to be a cunt to take one in, and I wished to dissolve in spunk.

Lord Rasper swelled and swelled, stretching every fold of

my cunt, his hands clasping round my body and frigging my clitoris so rapidly that I spent first, shooting a perfect flood of juice into his hands, which he rubbed on my mount and over my belly. Perhaps, indeed most likely, my excited looks told them all I had spent, each one stiffened and swelled more and more, till I felt the simultaneous rush of spunk from them all the same moment. Herbert nearly choked me with his profuse spendings, which I amorously sucked down to the last drop. My bubbies were deluged with sperm, which also clotted the hair under my armpits, whilst the Captain and the General shot out theirs all over my neck, shoulders, and arms, the warm clots falling on my excited flesh seemed so many darts of love pricking me all over, and the delicious, piquant, rather fishy aromatic odour of so much boiling sperm added to the intoxication of the senses, and to pile up the agony of bliss my darling Rasper shot such a stream of boiling hot spunk up to my very vitals, that my teeth almost clenched in the intensity of the excitement, making poor Herbert cry out in real pain, which was fairly drowned by the groans and cries of the others as they almost dropped from the excess of their lubricity.

When at length we could look round we found the rest of the company carried away by their emotions, each bridesmaid's clothes and petticoats were turned up, showing the silk stockings and primrose or mauve shoes, whilst their drawers, &c., were masses of lace and frillings.

"Miss" Gordon's* good-natured hand was caressing the prick of her partner, who in turn had his hand on her fine cock-clitoris, as it stood out from her drawers and a nest of black hair shown through the opening.

* Whether the quotation marks are indicative of a tongue-in-cheek reference to the real gender of the participant is unknown. It is just as likely that it is merely one of the many typographical errors found in the source text.

The superb Italian girl had everything off, displaying the magnificent swell of her arse; the slightly olive-tinted skin making a beautiful contrast to those fairer skins around her; her whole belly from the navel downwards was a perfect forest of silky black hair, from which stood out a famous clitoris, eight or nine inches long, and as thick as a man's wrist, its red dark-looking head already glistening with thick pearly[122] drops of spendings, which her partner was very busy rubbing up and down the shaft, whilst he[123] postillioned her bottom behind with the other hand.

The Russian lady could also be seen mock-modestly trying to prevent her partner from finding her clitoris, declaring it was too shameful to presume upon such liberties, that she felt overwhelmed and shocked by the sight of so much indecency all around her, &c., but he soon tore open the envious drawers and exposed in triumph as fine looking a cock as any male could wish to have, set off by a bed of dark-red hair around its root. Her pale face blushed quite scarlet, and she hid [her] eyes quite shamefaced, as it were.

Each couch or alcove had its couple of lovers, and where any real resistance was shown, Selina and Isabel made themselves very useful in helping to render them powerless to resist or baffle the attacks of the gentleman's prick.

Little Miss Power, a lovely little darling, found herself struggling with a young officer of the Guards, who had the smallest prick in the club, but yet not one to be despised by a virgin, seven inches being no joke to a small tight-wrinkled, brown arse-quim like hers.

"Get away, Sir; you shan't touch me!"[124] she screamed, giving him quite a smart slap in the face, as he tried to raise her skirts.

This made him rather angry; he tossed her on to a couch,

and Isabel helping to hold the little vixen down, soon had up her clothes, so that he could bury his face in the slit in her drawers.

"By Jove!" he exclaimed, "this little devil has got a cock as big as mine. I'll just suck it, and see if her modesty will prevent her spending."

Saying which he fairly rent off her drawers, and Isabel removed everything else in[125] spite of all she could do. It was a most exciting scene, independent of what else was going on around, in fact, most of us were too fascinated by the sight to think of our own business till Miss Power's was settled. He took her clitoris in his mouth, and somehow her legs clasped him round his neck, whether to squeeze him in rage, or induced by the strange feelings his tongue and lips would produce, we know not, but we could see his finger trying to ravish the tight little hole behind, and thus add to her confusion.

He soon made her come, and after sucking up some of her ambrosial cream, took away his mouth, and treated us to a sight of the bubbling spunk still oozing from the head of her distended clitoris. Her whole frame now squirmed and twisted in response to the flame he had raised in her blood. She shut her eyes and bit her lips till the blood came, as she lay gasping and half conscious from the excess of her libidinous emotions.

Seeing this he quickly divested himself of all his clothes, and his cock being rampantly impatient he took her legs under his arms, and bending them, with the knees nearly up to her bosom, a friendly member knelt down and applied some cold cream to the head of his prick, and also to "Miss" Powers's tight, brown, wrinkled hole. Her dark red roses lay scattered on the floor, fitting emblems of the ravishment she was about to suffer.

His friend now directed his prick straight to the mark, and the first thrust was so strong as to awaken his victim to the sense of the fresh attack on the defences of her rear virginity.

"Ah, ah! Oh, oh!" she screamed, twisting her arse to baffle him, but in vain, as the friendly hand of Mr. Inslip kept him from losing his place. How his eyes gleamed with fiery passions, as he leant forward, and almost savagely took one of her beautifully rounded bubbies as far between his lips[126] as possible, and, I believe, actually bit her in his passionate ardour.

"Murder; he's killing me. Oh, oh! Help! Murder! Help!" she screamed again; but in vain, he was biting and fucking at her arse-quim as well with all his strength, getting in. Little by little, till just as fainted with the intense agony, his balls[127] banged against her arse in triumph, at the complete success of his assault.

Now, conscious of complete possession, he gave up biting her bosom, on which we could see several drops of blood where his teeth had been, and raising his body off her, still held one leg under his arms, letting the other rest over without other support than his thigh.

Evidently his prick was revelling and throbbing in the full enjoyment of the tightness of her lovely arse-quim, which even the spectators could see spasmodically twitching and contracting on his prick, by which it was gorged to repletion.

Presently Isabel brought her round by the powerful club smelling bottle which had been held under her nose, and seeing his inamorata open her eyes, he commenced to pat and caress her finely-shaped posteriors, telling her what pleasure she had given him, asking her pardon for all the pain she had suffered and, promising she should now feel all the heavenly delights of love, only to be felt by a girl when she is well fucked.

"You have hurt me horribly!" she sighed, in a low voice. "But now your distended palpitating instrument fills me with the strangest sensations. My arse clings to it in spite[128] of my will; my blood is on fire! Oh, oh, oh! Push a little to see if I can bear it; but, oh, you are a darling, man!"

Withdrawing his prick a little, quite big drops of blood-stained mucous oozed from the tight orifice, which sucked him in quite ravenously, as he pushed[129] in again. Three or four strokes roused all the warmth of her nature; her eyes flashed with responsive passion; she addressed him in every endearing term she could think of, until she grew quite bawdy in her expressions, using words no one would have given her credit for having heard, much less learnt the use of.

"Oh, fuck me; oh, bugger. Shove your splendid prick into me and split me. Frig my cock darling. Suck my titties! and, oh, do fuck me well!"

Then again—

"How you stretch and fill my cunt. Oh, oh! I'm coming, dear; spunk into me now. Fuck—fuck—fuck! I'm done. Ah, ah! Oh, oh!" as she went off into a faint from excessive pleasure.

Her arse-quim, held him so tightly that after he had spent and thoroughly enjoyed the contractions of her arse-cunt, as it tightened yet more and more on his delighted prick, he had quite a trouble to withdraw, and when the swelled head of his John Thomas* was at length extracted, it was with a plop, just like a champagne cork.

I had the Count fuck my arse-quim most deliciously; he made me feel[130] all the delights none but[131] a woman can experience who has her cunt so deliciously filled and stretched to

* Slang for penis. See "The Burial of John Thomas" from William Lazenby's clandestinely published periodical *The Pearl* (1879-1880) See also *The Sins of the Cities of the Plain*, p. 48

its utmost capacity, and her vagina full of rampant prick. His fine pego renewed all the voluptuous feelings, and made me fancy I again had six pricks to manage. His spendings shot up to my very vitals, and my own clitoris spunked copiously into his frigging hand.

Every one in the room now had a partner; the examples of Miss Brompton and Miss Power had such effect that the other bridesmaids submitted to their fate with a loving resignation quite beautiful to witness, especially when once a prick had got into them.

Signora Diva was insatiable; she would imitate the brides and enjoy herself with six men at once, and chose my husband for her rear rank man on account of the very splendid proportions of his manhood; she had my clitoris in her mouth; a gentleman on his knees to frig hers[132] for her, one in each hand, and also under both armpits.

We drowned her in sperm, and each one of us took a turn to fuck her ever craving arse-cunt, and when we spent over her body she gathered it on her hands, licking her fingers with the greatest possible gusto and lascivious abandonment.

Miss Mostyn lost all her proud looks when once a good prick melted its tallow into her enraptured bowels.

Mademoiselle Fatima even surpassed us all in her magnificent and hot sodomitic lust, for she conceived such a passion for the Russian Natica, whose thick prick-like clitoris had taken her fancy, that she insisted on having that girl fuck her arse-quim, whilst she herself buggered Lord Arthur who had Miss Power straddling over his neck, so as to allow Fatima to suck her clitoris, and frig Mr. Inslip and the General, whilst two others fucked her under the armpits. You should have seen her wriggle her splendid arse (it was a marvel of expansive beauty, with snow white and plump buttocks), as she rammed her excited cock-clitoris into his Lordship's delighted bum-hole. This was a regular spermatic orgie; she sucked and licked every drop she could get, and almost devoured little Miss Power's fine clitoris in her frantic efforts to extract the last drop of honey from its stem.

Now Mr. Inslip withdrew a curtain and revealed to our view in a recess a lovely [painting]* of a gladiator in the act of sodomising his victim, the latter being in the very agonies of death from wounds inflicted by his conqueror who was now crowning his triumph by pushing his enormous prick into the tight arsehole of his captive, as he firmly held him by the haunches, every muscle of the dying youth could be seen rigid in the throes of death, and his stiffened prick in the very act of emission, as it is said to do with every strong man who dies a violent death.

Such a life-like representation fixed all eyes in a spell-bound gaze, till he presently touched a spring, which made it slide back into the wall, leaving the entrance to a magnificently furnished room beyond.

"Now for "La Bague de Sodome,"† he said loudly, "every one must enter in a perfect state of nudity, as the gentlemen have to adjudge the prize of beauty to the girl who has the whitest, finest, largest, fattest, plumpest, and the best shaped arse and the tightest little hole," displaying, as he said so an exquisite wreath of pricks in gold and enamel.

We had by this time very few garments to dispense with, and, as we entered, we found our male partners seated in a ring on a circular divan, in the centre of the apartment.

All their pricks stood proudly erect as we marched round and round the circle. Presently they knelt down, and each one

---

* There is a word missing in the source text. Judging from the description immediately following, we can conclude that it is likely a description of a painting.
† The Ring of Sodom. This does not appear to be a reference to anything in particular.

caught the lady nearest to him, and proceeded to examine all their charms, thrusting their tongues into our arse-quims, handling and frigging our clitorises, feelings our bubbies, passing their hands over the expanse of our buttocks, as if to take measures of the proportions.

Fatima had an exquisitely pear-shaped arse, but was rather eclipsed by the plump "apple shaped" butt[133] of La Diva, whom many thought would gain the prize.

Miss Mostyn had a lovely, white, plump, bottom, rather between the two styles of posterior beauty. All her pride seemed fairly aroused as she submitted such magnificent charms to the general inspection. Lord Arthur was quite fascinated with her, and seemed quite to over-look the luscious and loveable Laura, his bride; but my husband, who seemed to be chairman, in virtue of his enormous prick, put it to the gentlemen if Lord Arthur's bride was not most entitled to be crowned with the wreath.

"Look," he said, holding her admiringly before him, "is there another with such a glorious Venus-Callipyge contour; reclining or standing, which of them can show such a lovely waist; such expanse of bottom. Look at the white, round, plump buttocks, and the swelling roundness of her hips, where not an angle can be seen. Then her cock-clitoris is almost an inch longer than any other; but above the tight-ness and heat of this lovely wrinkled arse-quim of hers, it is only equalled by its unrivalled elasticity, and its throbbing squeezes; see, it grasps my finger just as tightly as it would my prick. Lady Laura, you are the 'Queen of Sodom' for the present; no one can gainsay that!" as he placed the wreath on her head.

There was just room for the twenty gentlemen on the divan, as they nearly touched each other, and made a perfect ring, each one kneeling on the divan, and drawing a lady's arse to him, they all drove their stiff, hot pricks into the tightfitting arse-quims, which quivered and throbbed on their rampant cocks. Nothing now could be heard for a minute, but the suggestive smacking and flapping of bellies and balls against the arses of their partners, with cries of gratified lust and enjoyment.

Lord Arthur had Miss Mostyn; Herbert was in me; Rasper, of course, had Laura; and the Count's prick revelled in the arse-quim of Fatima. Each male frigged the cock-clitoris of his female partner.

Cries of delight and ecstasy resounded all [around]* the ring.

"You love! Oh, fuck me quicker, you darling, bugger! bugger! bugger! me. Shove it into me. Make your quim throb on my delighted prick. Oh, oh, heavens, how splendid. You quite touch my heart, dearest!" I heard Laura exclaim to my husband; whilst Herbert's movements equally thrilled every drop of blood in my veins, and thus with shouts of ecstasy we all came together in a glorious spend; the clitorises spouting their cream of love over the busy fingers of the gentlemen, who frigged them so excitedly.

I felt my partner rubbing my spunk from his fingers on to his own prick, as it poked in and out of my tight hole behind; this added to the piquancy of our emotions.

A gamahuchade followed, our partners reclining us backwards, with our arses well out on the divan, and going from quim to quim, like bees in search of honey. For my part, I can only say that such a succession of sucking lips and tongues made me again furious with lustful desire. We turned round upon them, and sucked their glorious pricks, tickling their balls and postillioning their arses[134] till they were like ourselves, beside themselves for a fuck.

---

* The source text is missing a word here. I have inserted 'around' as the most likely descriptor.

Lord Rasper again took, "La Rosière de Sodome," as he called Lady Laura exclaiming, as he did so.

"Now, I await the challenge of love from those lips I love so dearly."

"Then listen to the voice of love," replied her lady-ship, as a luscious resounding fart literally rolled from her bowels, as she presented her arse in front of his tremendous huge stiff prick.

"You must feel more loving and randy yet, my dearest lady," said his lordship, who had armed himself with a splendid looking birch rod, "This will warm that splendid arse of yours, and draw the blood down to the parts of love, till you feel[135] the fire of desire tingle through every vein of your body. There—there—there. How do you like that, eh?" as we could hear the switching cuts, which made her fairly writhe under the stinging impact on her flesh, which first flushed, then got deeper red, till we could see the bursting weals, with little dew drops of the vital fluid, just oozing from the broken[136] skin.

Lady Laura writhed and moaned with pain, which she suppressed as much as possible for a minute or so then a strange flush of excitement gradually overspread her face. The sobs turned to sighs of pleasure, as his lordship kept up an energetic flagellation, and we soon heard her amorously calling out for him to fuck and bugger her at once.

So impaling her arse-quim on his magnificent prick, he stood up with her, fixed as she was, and quivering with voluptuous emotion at finding herself again spitted, and filled to the utmost capacity of her arse by his glorious weapon. Stepping out a few paces he and his partner knelt down, and stopped for Lord Arthur, who took up Miss Mostyn in the same way, and placed her behind my husband, and handing her a rod, she amply repaid Lord Rasper for the flagellation he had inflicted on Lady Laura, skinning his buttocks with her stinging strokes, till he begged her to impale him on her splendid cock-clitoris, which, as stiff as ivory, was soon linked in his longing bottom. Then Herbert placed me behind Lord Arthur, and I repeated the flagellation ordeal till he begged pitifully for my clitoris to fuck and bugger and comfort his poor arse.

One by one the couples joined on behind, each going through the ceremony of birching the arse in front till [they]* begged to begin the enculade†, and at length we formed one complete Chapelet de Sodome‡ of forty enraptured links, moving in one wave of lust to the stroke of Mr. Inslip's baton (his prick) by which he marked time, for their backward and forward motions.§

No tongue can tell the lubricity excited by this volup-tuous combination. Each one seems to fuck and be fucked at the same time by every loving link in that chain of erotic passion.

Exclamations of endearment and ecstasy burst forth all along the line—

"You love. You dear. How your darling prick fills me with pleasure, &c."[137]

Some gave vent to long-drawn deep sighs. Others fairly groaned from excess of feeling.

"Oh, oh! How lovely! How delicious. Oh, fuck! Oh, spend, now! I'm coming again. Ah! Oh! oh!" &c., &c., intermingled with sobbing and screams.

We spent in thrills, which seemed to last so long the flow

---

* A word is missing in the source text. I have inserted 'they' here, though others are equally plausible.

† French for bugger or ass fuck.

‡ Rosary of Sodom.

§ This is, presumably, the "still more filthy and impossible" act Ashbee referred to in his entry on *Letters*.

into our bottoms being answered by a shooting emission from our cocks into the tight quivering quims which linked us in front, the line sways from excessive emotion; we clench each other with extra ordinary rigidity in the delicious agony of the moment.

Each prick swells bigger than ever as the excited sheath closes yet more tightly upon its beloved prisoner, and is so reluctant to let go the delicious morsel that when the line is broken up, the successive withdrawal of forty pricks—plop—plop—plop all along, finishing with a deep sounding report as Lord Rasper withdraws his glistening magnum from the tenacious arse-quim of his beloved Laura, it sounded[138] like a fusillade, especially as it was succeeded by a series of spermy farts from the tight wrinkled orifice.

Each one vied with the other in their ardour to lick up the delicious tricklings from each other's quims, which still quivered and throbbed as they gave out gushes of the imprisoned spunk, which had been accumulating all the evening.

This was the end of the orgie, and all paired off in couples to spend the night in separate bedrooms, where they could renew in privacy all the voluptuous delights of the previous evening.

As luck would have it, Fatima and the Signora Diva made a pair, and I will relate the finish of their erotic exploits just as I had it from the Italian girl's lips the next day.

Fatima, after drinking a big glass of champagne, threw herself on the bed, all naked as she was, with her long false hair looking like a dishevelled wild Bacchante, exclaiming—

"What luck, Darling Signora, to have you for my bed-fellow. Come, quick, and put your bottom over my stiff cock-clitoris, and make your own spend all over my belly and bosom, and squirt its hot spunk into my mouth."

She had a lovely cock-clitoris, which filled my arse-quim

most deliciously, and such was the heat of her nature, and the strong fancy we both had for each other, that we very soon came to the acme of bliss, notwithstanding all the excesses we had previously indulged in.

My spendings squirted out with such force that they went all over her neck, and even into her mouth, which she opened to catch all she could; her hand frigging me with a lightening touch (but with the most delicate manipulation imaginable, which adds so much to the delights of masturbation by a female hand).

Meanwhile her prick was shooting a torrent of love juice into my enraptured arse and entrails, which quivered and contracted on her delighted cock till the last drop had been sucked up far inside my bowels.

"How big a prick could you take, Diva?" asked the Circassian. "There are Paris made dildoes of all sizes kept in every room of this place. Will you be a man, and put on the biggest and most monstrous one that you can find in the box that is under the bed?"

The Signora was willing enough, and soon stood equipped with a huge monstrous hard india-rubber prick, thirteen inches round, large enough to satisfy the most craving of arses, and as big as any stallion's tool.

It was firmly strapped on, and looked perfectly life-like, as she held it proudly erect in her hand, but what a terrible monster it was.

Fatima lay on her back, panting and sighing with hot desire, her flushed cheeks and big open lustful eyes so plainly[139] telling the fire of passion which raged in her heated veins and throbbing hot arsehole.*

* The narrative voice switches from La Diva's mediated first person account by Eveline to third person, confusing the scenario by making it seem as though Eveline had witnessed the scene herself.

La Diva stooped over her to arrange a pillow under those lovely pear-shaped buttocks, kissing and sucking as she did so the lovely cock-clitoris which stood up from Fatima's belly, surrounded at its base by a forest of black silky raven curls which adorned the swelling mount.

"Now, fuck me, darling. I'm dying to be stretched and filled by the biggest prick you can put into me! Never mind my cries or groans, you can't hurt me more than I'm resolved to bear."

The dildoe was warmed in warm water, and the huge bollocks were filled with almost half a pint of hot thick cream before Diva had strapped it on: then putting some vaseline on its head and all along its length, she knelt upon the bed between the outstretched legs of the longing Fatima, bringing the huge head of the instrument to the dark-brown tight wrinkled looking orifice of her arse-cunt, and pushed vigorously, making a lodgement of about an inch.

Fatima was so madly excited that she threw her legs over the Signora's loins, and clasping her tightly in her arms, sighed—

"Fuck me; fuck me, quick, you darling. I want to feel your grand cock filling and gorging my arse to its utmost stretch, splitting me up, and spouting its spunk up to my heart."

In response the Signora made a tremendous effort to push in, the dildoe forcing its way a little further at every thrust.

Both girls were mad with desperate passion, the one to achieve, and the other to endure the voluptuous sacrifice.

Poor Fatima, the tears streaming from her eyes, and her face distorted by the excruciating agony caused by the tearing, rending force of La Diva's monstrous hard india-rubber[140] prick, clung to her ruthless ravisher yet more convulsively, kissing her and even making her teeth meet in the flesh of the Italian's[141] shoulder.

"You split me! You rend me! Fuck me! Fuck! fuck! Bugger me well, you randy devil. I'd rather die than beg for mercy; Push—push—A—h—h—re! It's in at last!" she exclaimed, with another long-drawn, "Oh, oh, oh!" seeming to faint into an unconscious state for about a minute, then both of them wild with passion plunged into a tremendous bout of fucking, screaming with ecstasy, as the thrilling shoves went right up Fatima till the balls of the machine flapped outside her arse-cunt.

"Fuck—fuck. Shove the balls into me. Oh, spend now. Spunk into me, you darling. Down me! I'm coming. Oh, oh! Oh! oh! Ah—re—re—re!"[142]

La Diva was also carried away by the tremendous excitement, as she screamed and ground her teeth whilst one of her hands grasping both their cock-clitorises, frigged and rubbed them together between their bellies, the united jets of spendings flying all over their mounts, and round their navels right up to their bubbies, in fact they were covered and sticky all over with sperm.

"You darling! You love! I'm coming too. Heave up your arse. Nip my prick. How splendid. My God, what a fuck! Ah—r—r—re!"[143] as she touched the spring so as to inundate Fatima's cunt with the delicious creamy emission.

Both fainted from excess of hot lust, and such unwonted exertions.

Fatima's arse-cunt, as she lay in the arms of her companion, holding, throbbing, and squeezing the dildoe in its still longing sheath, the folds of the inner parts clinging to it with that unsatisfied grasp so delicious to a gratified prick which has just spent its juice, and lies soaking and revelling in the after lethargic enjoyment, and gloating in the beloved and heaving darling below.

Thus lay the two lovers[144] till they recovered their senses, when, after a few gentle moves, La Diva managed to withdraw the dildoe, the distended sphincter of Fatima's arsecunt collapsing with a loud plop, as the instrument was slipped out, all covered with a mixture of blood and creamy mucous, which too plainly told the havoc which had been done within.

Dear Louis, this was the conclusion of the famous night's orgie.

You must come up to town soon, as the Club propose to give another ball soon, at which all the bridesmaids and the same company will be present again, and one or two charming novices are going to be initiated into the Club, there are also going to be some "spiritualistic" dark séances got up.

A most notable programme is being prepared, so I trust you will not fail to be here.

Believe me, as ever your old pederastic fucking friend,

EVELINE.

END.

NOTES

1 Whorship could possibly be a misspelling of 'worship' or, alternatively, 'whore-ship', which would constitute a neologism since it appears in no dictionary of English.

2 gentemen

3 susfain

4 of

5 of

6 fannys

7 docoration

8 roud

9 Ball

10 westry

11 genlteman

12 a a

13 ang

14 or

15 eock

16 ladyhip's

17 its

18 ereamy

19 snsertions

20 veapon

21 altrough

22 feel

23 prevated: 'pervaded' makes the most sense in this context

24 betweed

25 tittilating

26 musele

27 bis

28 fell

29 An errant apostrophe appears after 'could' in the source text.

30 its

31 affraid

32 Quotation marks are omitted for Eveline's response in the source text.

33 its
34 failling
35 velvetty
36 it's
37 und
38 I have preserved the original quotation marks since it is unclear whether the second part of this thought is a quote or simply the narrator's own addition.
39 get
40 This confusing double possessive has been preserved.
41 shoiwng
42 Opening quotation marks are omitted in the second part of Eveline's entreaty in the source text.
43 sobing
44 quie
45 be
46 tonching
47 she
48 cass
49 fell
50 for
51 Multiple quotation marks in this passage were omitted from source text.
52 'To effect' is repeated in the source text.
53 annointed
54 Closing quotation marks mistakenly placed after 'maddening!' in source text.
55 heading
56 burried
57 as
58 I'Ill
59 fell
60 very
61 tongueing
62 priek
63 streching
64 fell
65 ail
66 burried
67 suched

68 burried
69 carressed
70 your
71 in
72 pricc
73 occured
74 Question and quotation marks missing in source text
75 its
76 An erroneous question mark appears in the source text here
77 ;
78 I'am
79 Opening quotation marks omitted in source text
80 smoking,
81 mine,
82 affraid
83 transcendant
84 you know.
85 Closing quotation marks omitted in source text
86 carressing
87 "with an assumed shiver of emotion," If I do...
88 how
89 plumness
90 mal formation
91 at
92 postilloning
93 Closing quotation marks omitted in source text
94 hairly
95 will
96 kissing the cunt of the floor of the cabin
97 occured
98 Royal
99 its
100 it
101 whith
102 prostate
103 thit
104 kow
105 on'es self
106 tittillation
107 fell

108 excitement.
109 graceful as swan
110 Good-naturel
111 erotie
112 marriage.
113 stronge
114 lovered
115 oscultation
116 off
117 Closing quotations omitted in source text
118 me feel
119 strock
120 at
121 pego's
122 dearly
123 be
124 Closing quotation marks omitted in source text
125 is
126 lip
127 ball's
128 spit
129 bushed
130 fell
131 but,
132 her's
133 but
134 arse
135 fell
136 broked
137 Closing quotation marks omitted in source text
138 soundt
139 painly
140 india-rubbed
141 Italians
142 Misplaced closing quotation marks in source text
143 Misplaced closing quotation marks in source text
144 loyers

Appendix A—Some Actual Letters Between Boulton, Park, Lord Arthur Clinton, and Louis Charles Hurt

Ernest Boulton to Lord Arthur Clinton

4th December 1868

My dear Arthur,—

I am just off to Chelmsford with Fanny [Park]. We stay until Monday. Not sent me any money, wretch!

—Stella Clinton

[Several days later]

I shall be unable to come down on the 18th. Write at once; and if you have any coin, I could do with a little.

[Several days later]

My dear Arthur,—

We were very drunk last night, and consequently I forgot to write. . . . And now, dear, I must shut up, and remain affectionately yours,

—Stella

[Several days later]

My dear Arthur,—

I have waited for two hours for you, and do not like to be treated with such rudeness . . . I shall not return to-night— nor at all, if I am to be treated with such rudeness . . . I am consoling myself in your absence by getting screwed . . . Mamma sends her kind regards, and will be glad to see you on Sunday.

Frederick Park to Lord Arthur Clinton
                                    Duke Street
                                    Nov. 21 [*1869?*]

My dearest Arthur,—

How very kind of you to think of me on my birthday! I had no idea that you would do so. It was very good of you to write, and I am really very grateful for it. I require no remembrances of my sister's husband, as the many kindnesses he has bestowed upon me will make me remember him for many a year, and the birthday present he is so kind as to promise me will only be one addition to the heap of little favours I already treasure up. So many thanks for it, dear old man. I cannot echo your wish that I should live to be a hundred, though I should like to live to a green old age. Green, did I say?? Oh, *ciel!* the amount of paint that will be required to hide the very unbecoming tint. My "caw fish undertakings" are not at present meeting with the success which they deserve. Whatever I do seems to get me into hot water somewhere. But, *n'importe.* What's the odds as long as you're happy?

Believe me, your affectionate sister-in-law,

Fanny Winifred Park

———————

[*No date*]

My dearest Arthur,—

You really must excuse me from interfering in matrimonial squabbles (for I am sure the present is no more than that); and though I am as you say Stella's *confidante* in most things, that which you wish to know she keeps locked up in her own breast. My own opinion on the subject varies fifty times a day when I see you together. She may sometimes treat you brusquely; but on the other hand see how she stands up for your dignity of position (in the matter of Ellis's parts, for instance), so that I really cannot form an opinion on the subject. As to all the things she said to you the other night, she may have been tight and did not know all she was saying; so that by the time you get my answer you will both be laughing over the whole affair, as Stella and I did when we quarrelled and fought down here—don't you remember, when I slapped her face? My address is the same, as I do not move out of this street. I have enclosed a note to you in the one I wrote Stella last night. Good-bye, dear.

Ever yours,

Fan

Duke Street,
Friday

My dearest Arthur,—

I think I would rather you came in the middle of the week, as I fancy I am engaged on the Saturday (15th) in London, though I am not certain yet. If you came on Wednesday and stayed until Saturday morning (if you could endure me so long), we could all go up together—that is if I go. But please yourselves. I am always at home and a fixture. I shall be glad to see you both at any time. Is the handle of my umbrella mended yet? If so, I wish you would kindly send it me, as the weather has turned so showery that I can't go out without a dread of my back hair coming out of curl. Let me hear from you at any time; I am always glad to do so.

Ever your affectionate,

Fanny

Louis Charles Hurt to Ernest Boulton
Lochalsh, Inverness, and Wick
April 1870

I have told my mother that you are coming, but have not yet had time to receive her answer. I thought it well to tell her that you were very effeminate, but I hope you will do your best to appear as manly as you can—at any rate in the face. I therefore beg of you to let your moustache grow at once . . . even if in town, I would not go to [the Derby] with you in drag . . . I am sorry to hear of your going about in drag so much. I know the moustache has no chance while this sort of thing goes on. You have now less than a month to grow . . . Of course I won't pay any drag bills, except the one in Edinburgh. I should like you to have a little more principle than I fear you have as to paying debts.

———————

Appendix B—Text of the Penny Pamphlet *The Lives of Boulton and Park. Extraordinary Revelations* (first published May 1870)

MEN IN PETTICOATS. STELLA, THE STAR OF THE STRAND.

Among the many extraordinary cases which are from time to time brought before the public, none have created more sensation, or a greater degree of dismay in the respectable portion of the community, than the astounding, and we fear, too-well founded charge against Boulton and Park, and the

THE LIVES
OF
BOULTON AND PARK.

EXTRAORDINARY REVELATIONS.

THE TOILET AT THE STATION.

PRICE ONE PENNY.
Office : 5, Houghton Street, Strand.

outrages of which they have been guilty; the social crime, for so it is, which they have openly perpetrated, cannot be too strongly condemned.

We speak firmly, and without the slightest hesitation, when we say that the proceedings of these misguided young men deserve the heaviest punishment which the law can possibly award, for however their intentions may be explained, and it is extremely doubtful if they can be explained, we say at least there is one peculiar trait in the evidence which stands out in bold and audacious relief, and too plainly shows the base and purient [*sic*] natures which these misguided youths (for they are but little more) must possess. We refer to the entrance of Park into the retiring room, which is set apart for ladies at the Strand Theatre, who had the unblushing impudence to apply to the female attendant to fasten up the gathers of his skirt, which he alleged had come unfastened.

This act, simple as it appears upon paper, is sufficient in itself to arouse the just indignation of every true Englishman. We can now ask, and with a just cause too, what protection have those who are dearest to our heart and hearths: those loved ones whom we recognise by the endearing titles of mother, sister, wife or daughter.

Is it right, moral, or just that their most sacred privacy should thus be ruthlessly violated.

If every debauched *roué* can by assuming feminine garb enforce his way with impunity into the chambers set apart for our countrywomen, then we call upon law and justice to aid us in exposing these outrages upon decency.

Day after day, month after month, and year after year, we are startled out of our propriety by some fresh scandal, some fresh crime, the mere idea of which is more than sufficient to evoke the blush of shame upon the modest cheek. We are continually shocked and alarmed at the rapidly increasing follies and crimes of society, as they are laid before us in the columns of our newspapers.

And to those who are thinkers, it is, alas, too evident that the most revolting profligacy of the guilty cities of the plain, or the debauchery of ancient Rome during the days of Messalina and Theodora, could not possibly outvie many of the atrocious phrases of London life as they exist in the nineteenth century.

It is somewhat a mockery for us to boast of our civilization, when, within the last few years we have such cases brought before us as those of Mr. Bruce Ogilvy and his orgies at the house of ill-fame in Panton-street—of the vagabond Haymarket *café* housekeeper, Howard, and his wretched victim, poor Minnie Wilson—as Mrs. Beecher Stowe's Byron scandal—as the Mordaunt divorce cause; and last, though by no means least, we come to the subject of our pamphlet, the present charge against three *creatures* who, for a doubtful purpose, assumed the garb of females and preyed upon the unsuspecting; even if their designs were not of a more dark and terrible character.

These gentlemen? (heaven save the mark) rejoice in the respective cognomens of Earnest Boulton and Frederic [sic] William Park, their ages being twenty-two and twenty-three: the former describing himself as of no occupation, and the latter as that of a law student. As we have no intention of endeavouring to screen these persons (for in our imdignation [sic] we cannot apply a milder term), we copy from the newspaper reports their addresses, which are, in all conscience, aristocratic enough: Boulton resided at Shirland-road, Westbourne-grove, and Park at Bruton-street, Berkeley-square—their present residence, however, being at Her Majesty's House of Detention, and for the present they are guests of a paternal government.

It appears that on Thursday night, the 28th ultimo, that no little excitement was caused in the Strand Theatre by the entrance of two very handsome women, accompanied by a young gentleman, into one of the private boxes, in fact, the personal charms of these ladies were so great that they attracted general attention, and we have on good authority that more than one bet of no inconsiderable amount was staked between some of the regular habitués of this place of amusement, with the object of deciding to what nation they belonged. The general opinion throughout the house being that they were two fresh stars about to shine in the firmament of the demi-monde, and that their beauty, their fascinations, and their paid for smiles, would, before the London season expired, cause many a poor dupe to curse the hour in which he had been born.

These and other numberless conjectures received their foundation from the nonchalent [sic] manner in which these ladies leaned over their box, twirled their handkerchiefs, and lasciviously ogled the male occupants of the stalls.

How few in that vast assemblage thought that these creatures were but men in masquerade; that the lecherous leering and subtle fascinations, which, if displayed by a woman, are much to be condemned, but what words can paint the infamy of such hellish proceedings upon the part of men towards those of their own sex.

For twelve months have the police been watching these men-women, but for a far more lengthened period have these contemptible creatures followed their nefarious practices. Whether their object was merely a felony: extorting money from men whom, in their assumed characters, they might have inveigled into their room, or whether a capital charge for an unnatural crime of a dreadful description, will be brought against them, we cannot, from the vague nature

of the evidence, at present, say; but the worthy magistrate
having positively refused bail, though tendered, to any sum
required, together with the fact that upwards of forty letters
from various parts of England and Scotland, are in the hands
of the police, detailing the practices of those arrested, written
by those whom we presume to have been the dupes of the
prisoners; and, independent of this, the crown have a vast
quantity of witnesses, and information from private sources,
which have yet to be brought forward.

But, under the circumstances, we cannot do better than
quote the evidence as given by the principal witness:

Mr. Hugh Alexander Mundell was then sworn. "I live at 13,
Buckingham Palace-road. I am 23 years of age. I was taken
into custody at the Strand Theatre last Thursday week. I am
willing upon my oath to state what occurred at the Surrey
Theatre, where I first became acquainted with the defendants
Boulton and Park. I knew Boulton as Miss Stella, and by no
other name until I was in the Strand Theatre. I first made his
acquaintance on Friday April 22, at the Surrey Theatre. He
was with Park in the dress circle. I never saw either of them
before. They were dressed something like they are now
(gentlemen's ordinary walking costume). I went there alone.
I went to several places in the house, but principally to the
stalls. I was taking some refreshment at the buffet, and my
attention was called to them as being women dressed as men.
I believed them to be women. They went to a public house
outside together; then they went back to their seats. I followed them. They waited till the next part was over, then
they again went out. I followed them. They said, 'I think
you're following us,' in a joking manner. I said, 'I think we
are.' They said nothing, but leaned over the dress circle. They
did not go to their seats. We got into conversation. I don't
know what we talked about. After we had been in conversa-

tion a little time, I asked them if they would like to go behind the scenes. They said they would, and I asked the permission of Mr. Shelley the lessee, and he allowed it. We then went. I don't think there was anybody else. We remained about a quarter of an hour. We went back again into the theatre and saw the piece out, leaning over the back of the circle. They asked me, as we had lost the thread of the story by going behind the scenes, if I would go and see it again. I said I should only be too happy, but I could not go before Tuesday, as I was engaged. We soon left the theatre and walked on towards Waterloo Bridge. There were only we three. We parted at the bridge, and I chaffed them and said I thought they were women in men's clothes. I told them when they walked they ought to swing their arms. We parted, and I went towards the city and they went home. I don't know that either of them told me where he lived. I should not like to swear to it. At that time I did not know Boulton by any other name than Stella. I don't remember whether I knew their names that night. I made an appointment for the following Tuesday, the 26th April. I agreed to meet them at the Surrey Theatre. On the Friday I did not see anything remarkable in their conduct. I was only told they were women by a man who went with them to the public-house. I believed they were women then. They looked so much like women when in men's clothes that I was led away. I don't know what became of the man who spoke to me. There was another man; but I don't know his name. The appointment was made for the following Tuesday; but I did not communicate with them. They arranged to have a private box, and I was to meet them there. I believe they both said that. The next Tuesday at half-past eight, I went to the Surrey Theatre. I waited some time before they came. I then saw them come in dressed in female attire. Park asked me to go into their box. I went with him and Boulton into the box. They walked in together. I took with me two flowers, and presented one to each, and I went out to fetch some pins to pin the flowers to their dress. When I came in Boulton gave me a letter. I took out the letter in the box to read but it was too dark. The letter was torn up, after I read it, by Boulton and Park. Boulton told me to go outside to read it. I said, 'It was a good joke, and I did not believe it.' The letter was not torn up on that day. It looked to me to be a woman's handwriting. I don't know by experience. I'm not in the habit of corresponding with women. (Laughter.) I did not notice by whom it was signed. The contents of the letter were that they were two men, but I did not believe it. They said, "It is true; we are men." After this we went into the saloon, and while having refreshments Park got into conversation with a young fellow. I did not hear what they said. I asked Park if he had seen that young man before. He replied that he had not. I never saw the man before. On that occasion I only knew Boulton by the name of Stella. Park went by the name of Jane. We saw the end of *Clam*, and then Boulton asked me to send after their man Jack—the driver of their brougham. I ordered the vehicle to be brought up. I asked for Mrs. Graham's carriage by Park's direction. Park went by the name of Mrs. Graham. I conducted Park down to the brougham, and the other man escorted Boulton (Stella) down. We all drove to the Globe Restaurant, in Coventry-street, and got out there. We all had supper there in the public room. I paid for the supper first, but the other gentleman insisted upon paying his share of half. The prisoners asked me if they could drive me anywhere, and they drove me to Ebury-bridge, Pimlico, near where I lived. While we were having supper Park gave me his address as "Mr. Park," written down, of 13, Bruton-street. We left the Globe about twelve. I made a proposal to Stella? [sic] I asked him when I could call and see him, and where. I believed Boulton to be a woman, and said I could meet him at Park's lodgings on Thursday, and he said I should meet him. Boulton had told me that he lived somewhere in the country. I heard somehow that Boulton came from Ledbury, and that he was staying at Paddington. No reason was given why I was not to meet Boulton at his place. He told me in the course of the evening that he had not long been back from Edinburgh. I arranged to go on the following Thursday (the 28th) to the lodging 13, Bruton-street. I went there, and sent up my card by a little girl. My address was on my card. I was shown into a room in which Boulton and Park were dressed the same as I first saw them at the Surrey Theatre. When I saw them they were playing the piano. Soon after that they asked me if I had got the letter with me. I cannot say which of them asked me. I said I had. They asked me to give it them. I said I was not going. We had a bit of a tussel for it. They tried to get it away, but did not succeed. I then gave it to them, and they tore it up, and returned me the torn pieces, which I did not accept. We were making a tremendous row, and the neighbours went in and complained. One of the defendants played one piece on the piano in one room and the other on the piano in the next room. Park said he expected a gentleman. Subsequently two gentlemen came in, to whom I was introduced. I forget their names. They were talking constantly about performing and playing, and one of the gentlemen went away. Afterwards we all four went out, when Park went into a shop. Boulton said he had come up from Edinburgh, and was waiting for the arrival of a friend, when they intended going to Paris. He did not say who the friend was. We settled we should go to the Strand Theatre that night. Park went into the shop (Mitchell's) and took the box. I walked on with Boulton and the other gentlemen. Then Park caught us up. I think he said the name of Mrs. Graham. I was told by one of the defendants to ask for Mrs. Graham's box when I went to the theatre. We went to Chancery lane to some chambers. I did not go with them. Park went to the chambers and I went to a place to have a glass of beer. Boulton went with Park to the chambers, and I waited outside. They came out and said the man they went to see was out. They then got into a cab in Holborn, and I left them. I walked on and saw them again in Oxford-street, and they said it was all on my way, and I got into the cab. They went to a glove shop in Oxford-street. I did not get out of the cab. Park got out. They then went to a jeweller's shop, I don't know where, and they then went to Bruton-street. I asked them to let me take the cab, and they said they wanted it themselves. I said, 'Good bye,' and then they went upstairs to their chambers. I did not pay for the box, nor for anything at the glover's or jeweller's. I did not give any money to the defendants to pay either. That evening at eight o'clock, I went to the Strand Theatre, and asked for Mrs. Graham's box. I went into the private box, and remained there some time by myself. A gentleman came there. I knew him slightly. I never was introduced to him. I had met him in public places but did not know him by any name. I think he said his name was Gibb. I chatted with him. Some time afterwards the defendants came into the box. They were then dressed as women. We remained until St. George and a Dragon was over. The gentleman left the box before we did. He made some excuse to go. The defendants went outside somewhere, but I remained in the box. I believed Park's train was torn. This was before the piece was over. I never left the box till I went to fetch a cab for them. They left the box once. A stitch in Park's dress had come undone. They afterwards asked me to fetch them a cab, and as I was alone there I did. They gave me some address to go to. I gave directions to the

cabman to drive to Pall-mall, where I was going to get out.
The defendants behaved like ladies at the Strand. There was
nothing wrong there. I was told in the theatre by some
person, the gentleman in the box, that they were men. I said
I had my doubts very much about one, and was quite in a
myth about it. I certainly believed Boulton was a woman. I
said I never had been taken so in all my life. I thought they
had done this twice for a lark. The man Gibb was the one
who informed me. It may have been Gibson. I think he said
he lived in Bruton-street. I saw no other man than Gibb there.
I didn't see any man that I had seen at Bruton-street that day.
One of the policemen at the theatre told me that he did not
want the men, and that I might go off. I said I had done
nothing wrong, but I did not like to leave them, as I had been
with them all day, and I thought I could help them to get bail.
I found myself in a cab on the way to Bow-street. I don't
know how it was. (Laughter.) At the police-station the defendants were taken out, and I remained in the cab. I walked out
afterwards. At the station I gave my right name and address.
I don't remember what occurred at the station, whether they
gave their right names, &c., I was rather flurried. Up to that
time Boulton never gave me an address beyond that he lived
somewhere up at Paddington. I never was at 13, Wakefield-
street, in my life. I never saw the defendants more than four
times in my life. I never heard anything about that address. I
have told the court every place where I have been in company
with these men."

Thus far went the case, the sequel being that the prisoners
were remanded for another week. Of the criminal intentions
of these misguided young men there can be but little doubt,
for the evidence of the man Mundell is sufficiently clear to
prove the systematic working of the infamous plot.

We shall be much astonished if these people are not punished with the due severity which their conduct so richly merits, and we can only hope that no foolish leniency will be exhibited in this case.

That, at the present day, we should have in England a large per centage of our population who will not work, but prefer to prey upon those who do, I as fact as alarming as it is true.

It is this class of young men who are the embryo Redpaths, Roupells, and Higgs of the next generation; and it is certainly time, we think, that the members of both Houses should unite and pass a bill with the intention of compelling the idle and disrespectable to seek some means of employment, and not to haunt low taverns, live upon the prostitution of the unfortunate class, or glean a livelihood by billiard marking and sharping.

There are few families who have not a black sheep in their flock; and these black sheep form a very large portion of the community, and the injury which they do to society is immense.

We only hint at the picture we could draw if we dare. We leave aside the common, and, by comparison, the cleanly vices of our time. We are not speaking of broken commandments: of Belgravian mothers: but we point below our breath to other signs of commandments broken which are too sacred to be written; of man metamorphised [sic], not to "beasts that perish," but to beasts procuring their own perishment, body and soul together, of abominations by which lust defies disease as well as heaven and all manly instinct; of houses——, but we cannot, indeed, tell the truth; and less than the truth is nothing in presence of the frightful vices that mock Christianity and poison society in our midst.

Since the above was written we considered it desirable that we should direct the attention of the public to a letter from Mr. A.C. Shelly, the lessee of the Surrey Theatre, which gives a fair and candid explanation in regard to the manner in which his theatre has been brought so prominently forward by the press. We quote the letter:

MEN IN FEMALE ATTIRE.

TO THE EDITOR OF "THE DAILY TELEGRAPH."

Sir,

Will you allow me the opportunity of explaining publicly what has evidently been made a great point of in this case, at Bow-street, in regard to my theatre, and which has called forth remarks from many quarters especially reprimanding me for permitting strangers to go behind my scenes? I can only say that the defendants were allowed behind the scenes simply under a total misapprehension, and that while there they conducted themselves with propriety.

I am, Sir,

Your obedient servant,

A.C. SHELLY

Surrey Theatre, May 9

The above, written as it is by a London theatrical manager, is sufficient to prove to the most obtuse person in creation, that the base insinuations which have been hinted respecting this gentleman's establishment have no foundation whatever; the case, in point, might have occurred at any other place in the metropolis.

Space will not permit us to enlarge upon the case which we are now reviewing; what the upshot may be (as we said before) we cannot say, for though it is our painful duty to lash the vices of society, still we do not feel justified in prophesying to the ultimate disposal of Messrs. BOULTON and PARK.

CPSIA information can be obtained
at www.ICGtesting.com
Printed in the USA
JSHW050210291122
33866JS00004B/210

9 781941 147573